SHINE ON, PRAIRIE MOON

A Novel

Tom & Esther

Thank you for
your friendship
July 2021
Mel + Elaine

Dee LeRoye

BY: Dee LeRoye

In Loving Memory
of
Leslie and Helen Caldwell
Louie and Irene Caldwell

Shine On, Prairie Moon

ISBN Number: 978-0-9727056-4-6

Published By:
Dakota Rose Publishing
23725 260th Ave
Okaton, SD 57562
PH: 605-669-2529
Dakotarose746@goldenwest.net
Dee LeRoye on Facebook

Cover design by:
Mesa Jean

The prairie moon makes a path of silver across the Bad River. Somewhere, not far away, a coyote calls a lonely howl and is answered by a series of yips. A familiar shiver creeps over me then and I rise quickly from my place on the old fallen Cottonwood.

I miss them so much, my brown-eyed Daddy and the spirited little lady who was his match in every way. How I would like to tell them what has happened in the years since they left.

Yet, not for one moment would I bring them back from the joy of heaven. So I must wait my turn to go. For now, I will share their story.

For yes, this is their story, trimmed with my own ideas and imagination of how it all happened and how it might have happened, but perhaps didn't.

Their prairie moon keeps shining.

Dee LeRoye

Prologue

When Sister left the room, the little mother moved quickly to open the bedroom window. The month was December and she knew Sister would come sweeping back into the room and shut the window again.

"What are you doing to my brother, trying to freeze him to death?"

"But the doctor said he has to have fresh air."

"Doctors don't know everything."

The little mother smoothed the pillow near the face of her beloved husband. In a few short years, he had given her three little daughters and the babe who now stirred within her. They had laughed and loved and worked their farm, and now he was slipping away, going out of her life and into some faraway place called heaven.

He had given of himself to help neighbors survive the Spanish Flu epidemic of 1918. And now the flu was killing him. Already she heard the death rattle of pneumonia, the side effect of the flu that would take him from her.

Just yesterday a neighbor had stood in the doorway of the bedroom and the sick man, in one of his last lucid moments, made his request, "Look after Kate and the girls for me."

His body was hardly still in death before his mother and sisters made plans. As soon as the birthing happened in a month or two, they would send "that nasty Catholic girl who let our brother die" back to her family in Montana, taking the brat with her. The three little girls, who showed promise of being almost as perfect as their father, would be separated and brought up by the sisters. The farm would be rented out to help pay for raising the girls.

What these women did not plan for was a stubborn young woman who did not give up without a fight. She stayed on the farm on the South Dakota prairie with her little girls and no amount of whining, begging or threats swayed her.

On March 5, 1919 she gave birth to her fourth daughter. Katherine was the name she passed on to her tiny baby. Even at an early age she was called Kitty to the point where most people never knew her by any other name.

When Kitty was six years old, the man who had promised to "look after Kate and the girls," divorced his wife and married Kate. He moved on to her farm to help her raise her family. His name was Fred, but in this story he is known as Pop.

Kate and Fred buried their only daughter a few days after her birth. So they poured their hearts and ambitions into the only son Kate would ever bear. He was adored and pampered by his four older half-sisters, yet he grew to be a hard-working, honest farmer who was respected and loved by all who knew him.

Eighty-eight years and two weeks would pass after her birth before Kitty met the man who was her natural father. As she lay dying, her oldest sister bent over the hospital bed and spoke comforting words. "After you meet Jesus, Mom will take you to meet our Daddy. Won't it be wonderful?"

But I digress, for this is Kitty's story, beginning with her seventeenth summer.

CHAPTER ONE

Frank owned a car, and in 1936 a car meant freedom. But Frank loved her sister Twyla, not her, so for now she would remain a prisoner in the middle of a sea of grass; South Dakota prairie grass, which had struggled to survive in the not-so-nice Dirty Thirties while grasshoppers destroyed anything they could chew and the wind sifted topsoil into houses and made dirt banks over machinery.

So, other than walking, her only means of escaping the dry prairie would be Bronco, her cow pony. Now he stood with drooping head, dozing in the heat of late afternoon. He stomped at flies nipping his sturdy legs and his black hide rippled to drive the pests from areas where his swishing tail could not reach.

Even at seventeen, Kitty Kruse appeared small for her age. Petite, her mother called her, but one of her three sisters called her plain old dinky even though she stood at least an inch above any other member of the family, including Pop.

The day of open grazing still existed, meaning there were few fences and ranchers could graze their cattle anywhere close to their private land. Kitty herded Pop's cattle wherever grass was finally growing again. Herding had been her job for years, and she did not mind the work. She let the hours slip by unnoticed by reading any book she could get her hands on, often spending the lonely minutes lost in pages of fantasy. Books were hard to come by in those days, so Kitty often read a novel until she could repeat many lines from memory. Now, on this hot June day she finished reading her favorite western novel for the fifth time.

From reading those western stories she had concocted a tall, handsome cowboy for herself. He would come riding out of the Jackson Hole country of Wyoming on a splendid horse, preferably black, and would wear silver guns at his hips with a big white hat perched jauntily above his beautiful face. Good guys always wore white hats, didn't they? This cowboy would immediately fall in love; with her, of course.

She closed the book as she sat up. Scanning the western horizon, she imagined the Grand Tetons. The majestic mountains reached for the sky from the valley floor and the Snake River led the way to the lake, shimmering blue in the sunshine.

"Jackson Hole," Kitty murmured. "I'll go there to find my cowboy. Oh, he will be tall and broad shouldered. We will..." A green-headed fly, having pestered her most of the hot afternoon, landed on her nose. She swatted at him with her battered old straw hat, which bothered him not the least.

The cattle she was herding had spread out in all directions, seeking the best grass. Many were lying down for an afternoon nap, content to lie still, chewing cud with no apparent concerns. She noted even Bronco standing idle. The girl pulled up her legs so her elbows could rest on her knees. With head on arms, she closed her eyes and relaxed, again daydreaming of her cowboy.

She spent some time talking with her Lord, too. Was it right or wrong to ask for a handsome cowboy to take her away from Pop's tyranny? Could it even be possible for a young couple to make a go of living in these destitute times? Mom had taught her long ago to pray as if Jesus were sitting right there beside her and discussing whatever she thought important, even some things that didn't seem to matter much.

Large clouds were piling up in the western sky by the time Kitty rose to her feet. "Maybe we will get some rain tonight," she suggested to no one in particular, "shore we do need some. I've never known such a drab, hot summer. Rain might not be exactly exciting, but it would at least cool things off a little."

She propped the book in a fork of a lower branch on the only tree in sight. And then she started toward the dozing Bronco with intent to catch hold of the lariat she had earlier fastened to his halter. Instead of being sleepy as Kitty thought, the gelding watched her with alert eyes. He waited until she almost reached the end of the rope, and as she bent to pick it up, he trotted away, dragging it behind him. He stopped as soon as he was out of her reach, and each time Kitty attempted to snatch up the end of the rope, he trotted away again. Bronco turned his head to the side to avoid stepping on it and kept up the game. Exasperated and sweating, Kitty at last gained hold of the rope.

"Grin, you old rascal," she snapped with sudden impulse to use her end of the lariat on his rump. Instead, she coiled the rope and carrying it over her arm, returned to the tree.

She took Bronco's bridle from where it hung on a branch, slipped it over the cow pony's head, and fastened the throat strap. And then she unsnapped the lariat from his halter and hung it in the tree near her book. Grasping the reins and a handful of mane, Kitty swung up on the horse's bare back, catching her heel over his backbone and wiggling up to a point where she could sit upright. She took the book and the rope from the tree and moved off to gather the cattle for the trip home.

Bronco chose his own trail most of the time. The cattle moved toward the farm by habit and Kitty needed only to bring the stragglers. Again, she fell to dreaming, reliving the beautiful romance still surfing her brain. Now she laughed to remember how her heart pounded when Indians captured her hero, and how tears misted her eyes when she read of the beautiful woman weeping over her cowboy.

"I wish I were beautiful," she thought, rubbing one bare heel against Bronco's soft hide. The horse shied at Kitty's action with a leap to the side, then trotted ahead. Clutching the book and lariat, Kitty urged the gelding to a lope and headed away from the cattle. Her heart thrilled at the fast, smooth ride Bronco gave her. They came to a narrow gulch, which the horse sailed across without breaking stride. He raced down the creek bank and slid to such a quick stop Kitty gripped hard with her knees to keep from falling into the water.

"Too much riding the saddle lately," she scolded herself. "It's good for you Ginger demanded it today. You need some bareback riding practice."

Bronco waded out into the shallow water and lowered his head to drink. Kitty stared into the water, watching a tiny bit of tadpole as he darted here and there. She did not see the snake swimming toward Bronco's head.

Kitty felt the gelding leap once before she splashed into the water. For an instant she sat there in shock, then a giggle stole her breath away followed by an outright laugh. Her bottom had met with the muddy creek bed, while one hand still held a bridle rein and the book was clutched in the other. The lariat coiled up her arm.

"Bronco," she sputtered, "you old dummy. A water snake wouldn't hurt you. You didn't have to go piling me off in the muck. He would have swum around your silly, ugly mug and went on his way."

Her laughter ceased. Creek water dripped from the book.

"Oh no, I must have dunked it. Oh no, Ginger's book. She will be so mad. She will tell Pop and he will have my hide." Kitty rose sadly to her feet and waded out of the creek to where Bronco stood waiting at the other end of the rein.

After taking the ragged bandana from her neck, she spread the pages of the book and tried to blot the worst of the water from them. Already, there were dirty spots staining the cover and sticking the pages together. Tears dripping from her eyes did not help the situation at all.

A rumble of thunder from the west reminded her to get moving toward home. To make matters worse, the cattle had drifted over towards the road in the opposite direction of the barn and corrals. And, of all things, a Ford Model A vehicle puttered right down the middle of the road and would further scatter her herd.

She scrambled up on to her mount's broad back and put heels to his sides. As she neared the herd and the vehicle, she recognized the car to be Frank's, but she was puzzled as to why her sister's feller would be driving away from his sweetheart's home instead of towards it. When the car stopped, she rode on up to say "Howdy" and leaned over to do so, unmindful of her mud-spattered clothes.

"Aren't you going the wrong way?" she quizzed.

"Truthfully yes, wisely, no. We drove over to your place hoping to get in some fishing, but those clouds in the west could actually bring some rain. We don't dare be marooned in mud this far from home."

"Oh, I didn't even realize this is Sunday. Twyla did say something about you and your dad maybe coming fishing on a Sunday afternoon."

"Yes. Dad stayed home to look after Mom. She had a nasty flareup of her rheumatism. This here is my little brother. Perhaps you have met him before?"

She leaned further ahead to peer into the vehicle and found herself looking into dancing brown eyes. His warm smile made her very aware of her soppy, mud-spattered overalls, tattered old shirt and wind-snarled hair.

His smile...could he be laughing at her appearance? Anger crawled up her spine and peeked over her shoulder at the handsome young man. So finally the fellow she had heard so much about was no longer a stranger. Frank's brother Brice presented a face to remember. And quite an impression she must have made on him, too.

"P-pleased to meetcha," she stammered, and then looked back at Frank. "You probably want to get closer to home. Those clouds might have some rain in them."

"We are hoping to try the fishing expedition again next Sunday. You take care, now."

Kitty did not realize she was holding her breath until she released a sad sigh as the Model A chugged on down the trail. "Wow, no wonder Ginger talks about that young man every chance she gets. She saw him once in the store in Draper and thinks she is in love with him and he with her. I wonder what he thinks. I'll bet he doesn't even remember seeing her." She hesitated before adding. "I hope he doesn't remember seeing her, actually."

The wind came up even as she put Bronco into a fast trot to catch up with the herd, circle around and get them headed in the general direction of the barn and corrals of home. Even as she pushed stragglers to get moving with the rest of the cattle, the western sky turned into an ugly, dark mass, spreading with amazing speed halfway across the upside down bowl of her world.

She urged Bronco after the herd and moved homeward. The storm held no fear for Kitty, nevertheless she hoped to have the cattle inside a fenced lot or corral before the fury of the clouds was loosed.

Bronco, however, not being fond of storms, started with each clap of thunder. Kitty worked hard to retain her seat, hold the book and keep a watchful eye on the cattle. A few drops of rain spattered the ground, her arms, and bare feet while a blast of wind rushed through the prairie grass and brought a sudden chill.

"Hail somewhere, I'd say, by the feel of the wind."

She tucked the book in between the bib of her overalls and the front of her shirt. Noting the distance between the herd and the shelter of home, she talked aloud to no one in particular. "About a mile of rough country left now. And I suppose the milk cow's yearling steer will think this is a perfect night to cut back up the draw." Kitty urged Bronco into a lope, weaving to and fro at the rear of the herd, trying to urge the cattle to put a bit of speed in their gait. The chill wind caught and ruffled her dark curls and gusted as if trying to unseat her. Bronco seemed to forget his fear and fell to work hurrying the stragglers toward home.

The cattle moved into the lot just as the hail began. Kitty leaped off to close the gate, than ran beside Bronco to the barn where Ginger held open the door. A spattering of ice on his rump made Bronco leap ahead and through the door with Kitty at his heels.

"Boy, I'm glad that white stuff isn't any bigger," Kitty grabbed for breath as she faced her sister.

"That's the fastest I've seen you and Bronco move out in a long time."

"H-m-m." Kitty chose to ignore the remark and caught up the reins, then slipped the bridle from Bronco's head.

"There are still a couple cows for you to milk. I'm going to feed the calves."

"H-m-m," Kitty answered again. Milking ranked at the bottom of her favorite ways to pass time. "Whose cows?"

Ginger turned on heel to face her. "Yours."

"Sure, but who usually milks them?"

"I do. But you always get out of night milking. You wait until you know we are finished, and then you bring the cattle in. I figure since you are here, you can help."

A spark of temper burned along Kitty. "I will see you out here milking in the morning then. If I'm supposed to help at night, I'd say you ought to help in the morning."

Pop stood in the doorway, unheeded by the girls as Ginger turned on her younger sister. "You think you are so smart, Kitty. Well, there are a few people around here who do an honest day's work while you are sitting on your duff out in the pasture. There's a bucket," she pointed. "And a cow who needs milking right over there. Now, move."

Kitty deliberately fussed with the bridle before she hung the headpiece on a nail in the wall. She smoothed the reins and straightened the chin strap. Her eyes noted the saddle hanging on the manger, exactly where she had left it the night before. "Didn't ride today, huh?"

"What's it to you?"

"You ordered me to leave the saddle home because you were gonna ride. Well, I reckon I'll use the saddle tomorrow." Kitty stated, more to herself than to her older sister.

"Reckon you won't," Ginger snapped.

Just as Kitty reached for a milk bucket, a strange sensation of a book sliding down her pant leg made her gulp in panic. Even though she halted all movement, the tome peeked out.

Ginger noted the panic in her sister's face and followed her eyes to the floor of the barn.

She bent down and wiggled the book out of the pant leg. "Hey! What happened to my book? The rain couldn't do this much damage."

Kitty leaped toward her sister to snatch away the novel, but Ginger stepped out of her reach and laid it on a shelf.

"It just got a little wet," the younger girl said.

Pop's growl caused both of them to turn and stare. "I told you not to take a book along to the pasture. Now you have ruined it. Lot of carelessness."

Kitty swiped a milk bucket from its nail in a barn wall stud. Before she stomped off toward the milking pen, she said, "I do not have a place to carry anything when I don't have the saddle. You ought to have seen my sandwiches today. Bread and jelly all over inside my bib pockets."

"Go hungry for a few days," Ginger chided. "You could stand to lose a little of this padding back here," she swatted Kitty's backside.

"Cut it out."

Ginger laughed as she strutted away with Pop.

Kitty moved into the milking pen. The pungent smell of cows and hay greeted her. Her two other sisters were busy milking. Grace glanced up to smile a welcome at the younger girl, her hands and arms never losing their steady rhythm. The milk foamed and bubbled in the pail.

"Did you get hailed on?" Twyla asked from a darker corner of the barn. Again the even squirting of milk never hesitated.

"Not much," Kitty muttered. She perched on a stool near a cow, held the bucket between her knees and added to the rhythmic noise of milk streams making foam in buckets.

A change in the hammering noise on the barn roof told them the rain had lessened. Soon the rattle of raindrops stopped. By the time the girls finished the milking, puddles around the yard made up the only rainwater to be seen.

Kitty turned the milk cows into the corral. She stood in the doorway of the barn and inhaled the fresh smell of settled dust. "Come here, Grace."

The two girls stood in the doorway, looking at the rainbow arched across the eastern sky.

"Do you believe in God, Kitty?"

"Yes. You know I do. Isn't my belief the reason you sometimes ask me to pray out loud? But, anyway, how could anything so pretty just happen to exist if there is no God?"

"Remember so long ago at school when Mister Robinson told us about how the sun shines through the rain drops like a prism?"

"Yes, he said the prism is how science explains a rainbow. But he also said someone made the sun and rain to begin with and he told us how God used the rainbow as a sign of his promise to Noah."

"Anyway, I'm glad the earth will never be completely flooded again."

"So am I. We sure could use a slow, long, warm rain, though. This weather is hot and dry again for June. These thunderous little showers do not do much good for pasture grass."

"Guess I'd better go help Ginger crank the separator before she hollers for me, or just leaves the whole job for me to do." Grace started across the barn, and then called over her shoulder, "Mom made ice cream for supper."

"Oh yum. First ice we have used this summer, right?"

"Yes. The blocks are still hard as a rock, so if the old ice house can keep it so well, we won't lose our bedroom for a while."

Kitty turned back to the doorway. She and Grace had moved their old iron bedstead into the new ice house in early spring, happy to have a bit of privacy as well as a room in which they might stay cool during the heat of summer nights.

As she walked away from the barn, she could still hear the steady whine of the separator in the small room on the other side of the barn as her sisters turned the crank round and round, spinning the bowl and disks to separate the cream from the milk.

In the enclosed south porch of the farmhouse, she bent over the washstand to swish the dust from her hands and face. After drying on a rough, but clean, towel, she emptied the basin into the slop bucket, then refilled it from the water bucket.

In the kitchen, she set plates and cups on the table while her mother stirred potato slices in a cast iron skillet on the cook stove.

"Would you fill my kindling box, Kitty? There's enough fire in the range yet to keep water hot for dishes, but I'll need kindling to get the fire going in the morning."

"Sure, Mom." She went back outside to the little shed behind the house where she filled the kindling box with dry corn cobs and wood shavings. After she put the box back beside the cook stove, she carried out the water pail from the porch, which she filled at the cistern. While pumping the iron handle up and down above the platform, she enjoyed the creak and scrape of pipe and leathers, the rush and swirl of water filling the bucket.

For a minute she remembered the time she had called Ginger a nasty name because the older girl would not let her pump the water. Ginger let go of the handle, swung a fist and clipped the left side of Kitty's face, including her eye. Even now Kitty wondered if she would ever have full sight in the eye again. She knew she ought to forgive her sister, but somehow, she couldn't bring herself to do so. Maybe if her sister had said, "I'm sorry." Maybe not.

The problem was when she recited the prayer Mom had taught all her girls: when she got to the "forgive us our sins as we forgive those who sin against us" part. Maybe God would not forgive her if she didn't forgive Ginger.

The rest of the family had gathered in the house when Kitty entered with the brimming water bucket. She filled the enameled wash basin with hot water from the cook stove reservoir, cooled it slightly with cold water, and placed the basin before Pop, then stood by with the towel as he scrubbed his face and hands. He took the towel she offered without word, and she stepped back into the kitchen where Ginger and Grace were already seated at the supper table.

Mom and Twyla finished putting food on the table and took their places as Pop joined them. Ginger recited her usual table grace. "Come Lord Jesus, be our guest, and let this food to us be blessed."

Hardly a meal ever passed but what Kitty wondered what the meal would be like to actually have Jesus as a supper guest. But she soon dismissed the mental question as the family began to devour the food.

Kitty figured one could never get tired of Mom's cooking. Tonight there were fried eggs and potatoes along with a jar of green string beans from last year's garden, but what Kitty liked best was a thick slice of Mom's home baked, white bread with rich, yellow butter.

"What kind of jam is this, Mom?" Grace asked, spreading the bright preserve on her slice of bread.

"Juneberry. Frank brought over a couple jars."

"Yum," Ginger said, "he sure makes good jam."

"His mom made it," Twyla inserted while wishing she could hide the blush creeping into her cheeks at the mention of her sweetheart's name.

"You better learn to cook as good as his mom does or he will never marry you," Grace teased, biting into her richly spread sandwich.

"Who says I want to marry him?"

Grace opened her mouth to reply, caught sight of the sullen expression on Pop's face and shut her mouth again on her sandwich. Kitty compared her action to a fish and how he opens and shuts his mouth when he is pulled out of the water, but she'd never seen a fish eat bread and jelly.

"Save some food for Teddy," Mom suggested softly.

"Where is he, anyway?"

"Finishing the book Frank left for him to read."

"That is the dumbest book I ever saw. It has nothing but pictures in it and funny circles by people's faces with words in them."

"It's called a comic book. This one is called 'Cowboy Stories'."

Kitty was wondering why her little brother was allowed to be late for supper because of a book. None of his older half-sisters would have dared to do such a thing.

The subject changed when Ginger blustered. "By the way, where's my book, Kitty? I went back to pick it up, but it was gone."

"I, I'm not finished with it yet."

"Who do you think you are kidding? You always finish a book in a day. You ought to be more careful with other people's property."

"We had an accident." Kitty could not stop the tears welling up in her hazel eyes, "I didn't hurt your old book."

"You ruined my book, soaked in creek water, no less."

"Well, you're all wet yourself."

"Kitty!" It wasn't her mother or Pop who reprimanded her with one word. It was her three sisters, in unison.

Silence took over the room as the youngest of the girls downed the remaining food on her plate and laid down her fork. "Excuse me please," she tossed in her mother's direction, and then stalked out of the house.

There she found the wind whipping across the yard, cooling her hot face, twisting at her hair. "Some day. Some day she is going to say the wrong thing to the right person."

She stood at the edge of the porch, sucking in the night air, watching the clouds scuttle across the prairie moon. Stars were beginning to twinkle far, far away even as the last of the day's light faded.

Grace came to the screen door and coaxed. "Come back in, Kitty. There's ice cream, you know."

"She can't come in unless she promises to do the dishes," Ginger called.

"Go toot your horn," Kitty sassed as she walked back into the house, took her place at the table and devoured the heaping dish of frosty confection Twyla set before her.

Later she did help with the dishes. She dipped steaming water from the reservoir in the cook stove to fill the dishpan before adding a blob of Mom's homemade soap. Twyla and Grace helped by clearing the table, drying dishes and putting them away in the cupboard. Ginger had disappeared.

"Frank and Brice came here to go fishing this afternoon, but the bad weather scared them off," Twyla told the younger girls softly. "The whole family is coming over after Sunday School next week to go fishing."

"The whole family?"

"Yes. Frank's mom wasn't feeling well today. I do hope she is better and can come along next time. She's a very special lady."

"She cannot be nicer than Mom."

"No, of course not, and she's different from Mom. She's a teacher, remember, but she still keeps a neat house and even bakes bread. Actually, she owns a bread machine."

"A what?"

"A bread machine is a bucket with a wooden lid, a handle on the top and a twister dealie on the inside kneads the bread dough as you turn the handle. Rheumatoid arthritis has left her hands quite crippled, you know."

"I didn't know. What did Pop say about the fishing?"

"Nothing. He doesn't know yet. Mom will tell him later tonight."

Kitty stared into the dishwater. "I hope you all have fun."

"You can go, too," Twyla whispered. "Mom said staying here in the lot for one day won't hurt the herd at all. There's plenty of grass on the home creek yet. One day's grazing won't even be noticed."

"You mean I actually get to go fishing? We all get to go?" Kitty's voice rose in excitement.

"Yes. But you don't need to holler."

"I am not hollering," Kitty giggled in reply. "I hope I catch ten more Bullheads than old Ginger does."

"Oh, she won't catch any," Grace stated.

"Why, what do you mean?"

"She will be too busy trying to catch a fisherman instead."

Kitty scowled, wondering exactly what that meant. The other two sisters exchanged a knowing look, but offered no explanation.

Before the impact of what her sister actually meant could register in Kitty's mind, Ginger swept into the kitchen unaware of being the topic of discussion. "Pop and I are going to Draper tomorrow. Do you girls want anything from town?"

"Sure," Kitty replied. "Bring me a handsome cowboy, a white stallion and three chocolate bars."

"Where's your money?"

Kitty turned back to the dishpan. "You wouldn't bring all three to me if I did have the money," she replied, picking up the dishpan and heading toward the door. She swung open the screen door with her foot and crossed to the side of the step where she flung the dishwater out of the pan in a silvery spray. Then she walked back into the house. "You'd keep the goodies all for yourself."

"Only the cowboy. You could have the rest." The two sisters actually exchanged smiles.

"No doubt. Okay then, bring me a horse. I'd take a good horse over a man any day."

"No doubt."

"Come on, Kitty," Grace implored. "Play some checkers with me. When I asked Teddy to play, he said he had to go read his book again."

"Checkers are for winter time," Kitty replied, but she sat down across from her sister. "One game only, then I am going to bed. I'll appreciate the extra sleep I can get for the early return from the pasture."

Twyla was in the bedroom she shared with Ginger where she was likely writing a letter to Frank. Ginger watched her other two sisters play checkers.

"Are you going to buy groceries tomorrow, Mom?" asked Kitty between checker moves.

"I'm going to get them," Ginger smirked. "Mom has to get her sweet corn weeded."

"You could help me do the weeding and we could give Mom a break," Grace put in. "She ought to go and visit her relatives. She'll forget what they look like."

"Well, I'm going," Ginger snapped. "Mom can come along if she wants."

While Kitty waited for Grace to make a checker move, she studied her mother where she stood by the cook stove peeling eggs for tomorrow's salad. The lady was short and growing heavier with age, but Kitty knew without looking that her sweet face still radiated beauty. Her black hair showed no sign of gray. Where the rolled sleeves of her print dress ended, her arms were ivory, but her hands were strong and tanned.

Kitty's eyes moved from her mother to the others in the room. Pop sat in a corner of the living room with his feet up on a hassock, a curl of Camel cigarette smoke trailing around his head. Twyla, though not present in the room, presented an easy picture in Kitty's mind with her sweet round face, tiny feet, usually without shoes, her small body hidden in a flannel shirt and bib overalls, yet slender and softly filled out in the necessary places when she wore one of her few dresses. She was probably writing a letter to Frank. Ginger, next oldest, and Grace, were small people, too, and no bigger than Twyla. Kitty treasured the fact of being the tallest member of the family, standing at a towering five feet, two inches, taller even then Pop.

"Little people," cousin Dell had called them when they were young girls in school. Kitty wrinkled her nose at the memory. She wondered if ten-year-old Teddy would be slender and tall when he grew up. Likely not.

At last Grace moved her checker and Kitty's game tokens were trapped. She surrendered to her sister's kings.

Then she and Grace walked together through the night to their ice house bedroom. They made their way carefully down the stairs in the dark and undressed in the same inky blackness.

The long-sleeved flannel nightgowns their mother had made for them were lying on their pillows, not hard to find even without light in the room.

The bed felt soft and comfortable under Kitty's tired body. She found a few tender places where hail had pelted her, but nonetheless, she soon slept soundly.

She arose before the sun did. Dew lay heavy on the grass to wet her bare feet and soak her pant legs before she reached the house. Her mother was frying eggs and bacon at the cook stove when Kitty entered the kitchen. Removing one of the lids from the range, Mom held a slice of bread on a long fork over the open flame, and then spread the toast with butter to complete Kitty's breakfast plate of bacon and eggs.

"Mom, I reckon I ought to be able to get my own breakfast. You could get a little more sleep."

"Thanks, honey, but the morning is the best part of my day. Anyway, what's a half hour more or less of sleep? The family will be up soon. Your sandwiches are here on the cabinet. I used the Juneberry jam. I hope they won't be too messy. I hope you soon are allowed to use the saddle again and can tie the lunch bag on behind the cantle."

"Ginger didn't even use the saddle yesterday," Kitty complained, tucking a sandwich in each bib pocket of her overalls.

"Pop's been keeping the other kids busy. There isn't much time for joyriding," Mom stated as she tied the strings of the old, worn straw hat beneath her chin. "I told Ginger to buy a couple boxes of chocolate bars with the other groceries. I think we'd better keep at least one box in the new ice house, don't you?" Mom was smiling as she started out of the house to do chicken chores.

"Yes," Kitty replied, "we wouldn't want them to melt, but you do know there are a couple mice living in there."

"Well, mice need to eat too, don't they?" Mom led the way outside.

♪ ♪ ♪

The eastern sky glimmered in a maze of pink, blue and orange, changing constantly as the blazing ball of sun crept almost into sight. Kitty counted by habit as the cattle passed by her through the gate. Then she swung up on Bronco, her hand laced in his mane, her bare heel catching over his backbone, and her strong legs pulling her up on to his back. The horse turned and walked behind the cows.

"Ack," she murmured. "I should have led Bronco up by the corral fence and got on there. I've an idea I squished my sandwiches and spread Juneberry jam all over the waxed paper when I crawled on."

She spent the day being lazy, wading in the creek, exploring old draws with Bronco, hunting bird nests, which she inspected from a distance, but left undisturbed. Otherwise, she just sat and enjoyed her daydreams.

Relaxing in the warm sunshine, she dreamed of her cowboy. He'd come riding in from somewhere, fall madly in love with her and carry her away to some green valley. Of course he would be handsome, with blue eyes…well, maybe brown, come to think of it.

He would be kind and gentle, like Uncle George, her daddy's brother.

And he must be friends with Jesus. She had seen firsthand how being a Christian was not easy if one of the persons in a marriage did not love Jesus.

Of course, he wouldn't drink whiskey or use bad language. Why, Pop wouldn't even let them say "gosh" or "gee" because that was just as bad as the swear words he used.

Then her mood faded and she scolded herself, "Here I am, almost a woman, maybe I am a woman, even, and I'm sitting her pretending like a child. What good comes from dreaming impossible dreams? I am tied to my mother's apron strings, afraid of my step-father, longing to do something besides herd cattle until I am an ancient, old maid in a rocking chair with nothing and nobody to call my own." A sting of bitter tears bit at her eyelids.

Swiping them away she got up and busied herself by attempting to climb a steep shale bank above the creek. The soil crumbled under her feet, sending showers of dirt clods clattering and bouncing downward.

When she tired of climbing, she washed her face and hands in the stale, tepid creek water and ate her sandwiches. In spite of being a bit squished, the soft bread and sticky sweet jam were delicious to her mid-afternoon hunger. She noted the cattle resting too, most of them lying down, soaking up sunshine, chewing cud without a care. Bronco grazed nearby.

After the lunch disappeared and she had licked the last bit of jelly from the waxed paper, Kitty stretched under the lonely tree and laid her hat over her face to keep flies from crawling around there in search of Juneberry jelly.

She was bored. She wished she had asked Teddy if she could borrow the comic book for a day, but then again, after reviewing the episode with Ginger's book, she decided it wasn't worth the risk.

She woke to feel a tickle on her arm. Imagination said her cowboy must be tickling her with a feather. Soon he'd take away her hat and kiss her awake and she'd pretend to go right on sleeping for a long moment.

Then Kitty thought of rattlesnakes and could not prevent the tightening of her muscles. Slowly she removed her hat and turned her head, expecting any minute to hear the deadly buzz of warning.

Thankfully, the creature tickling her arm claimed the title of Walking Stick, and stepped proudly up and down her arm. When he paused, he did indeed look like a tiny stick. Kitty allowed him to proceed in his wandering, and then finally snapped him off her arm to the ground. "Just in case you happen to be a female, you are not welcome on my territory," she joked. "Anyone who would eat their lover must be quite dangerous indeed."

As she used her sleeve to wipe the cold sweat from her face, she muttered. "I'll take a Praying Mantis over a rattler any day, but I'd rather be bored then find my diversion in the likes of either one."

Dusk came before Kitty returned home for the night. She rode through the darkening shadows, thankful for a break in the heat of the day at last. Later in the summer, even the nights would be hot, the cattle stubborn and the flies pesky. Then life might be easier if she packed a bedroll behind the saddle and slept out on the prairie rather than driving the herd back and forth each day.

As she made her way slowly behind the herd toward the barn and home lot, she could picture her mother waiting up with supper for her. She hummed a tune she had heard Mom sing in appreciation for the life she knew. Out there somewhere across the prairie a coyote howled. Kitty turned toward the sound, and after a moment, whispered, "Someday I'll be as free as you. I will roam, too."

CHAPTER TWO

Kitty leaped out of bed on Sunday morning and began to dress before she remembered she was beginning a special day. The cattle would not be driven out this morning. Frank and his family were coming to visit and fish.

She thought about climbing back into bed beside the sleeping Grace, then thought better of the idea and went to help her mother.

Bending beside the little woman, Kitty weeded the rows of tender garden plants until the sun rose. After a bit she got down on her hands and knees to crawl between the rows, pulling the offending plants out of the soil.

She chose to stay behind when her mother left to prepare breakfast. Later she saw the team being hooked to the scraper and was glad she had stayed in the garden. Ginger and Grace had been ordered to do the dreaded job of cleaning the barn.

When her stomach growled with hunger, Kitty went to the house for something to eat. Her mother was peeling potatoes. Twyla, already in her next-to-best dress, was removing bobby pins from her curls.

"Guess I'll wait now until dinner to have something to eat," Kitty said, but still cut off a chunk of raw potato. "I've just about finished weeding."

"Kitty, you need to fix your hair," Twyla called as the youngest sister left the house. "Don't you want to look pretty?"

"Nope." Kitty called back.

In the garden again, she bent to her task, creeping along on hands and knees between the rows. "Sure, I want to be pretty," she said to the carrots. "But the wind will blow away Twyla's hairdo, and who can fish in a dress?"

She worked on silently and was surprised when a voice called merrily over the fence. “What did you lose, little beggar girl with the muddy knees?”

“The love of my life. Do you suppose he could be hiding under a cabbage? I just can’t seem to find him anywhere.”

“If he’s under a cabbage, you’ll have to wait for him to grow up. That’s where they find babies, you know.”

“Oh really? You’ve been reading too many mush magazines.”

“If you think such information is what is in my ‘True Confessions’ magazines, you have much to learn, little sister.” Ginger entered the garden and walked up the row where Kitty worked. “Is this your last row?”

“Yes.”

“I’ll help you then.”

“You’ve worked enough already this morning. I saw you had to clean the barn.”

“Well, dinner is almost ready. We finished the barn. Grace’s poohed out and about half mad, but I’m still going strong. Excitement, I guess.”

“Excited about going fishing? Whyever?”

Ginger smiled coyly, “Ah, come on, sister. Surely you’ve seen Frank’s little brother.”

“That’s what you are all excited about?”

“Wouldn’t that be fun if two of us sisters could marry two brothers?”

“I thought we were going fishing, not to a wedding party.”

“Well, we never know, do we?”

Together they finished pulling the weeds from the row.

“If we get some rain now, Mom will have a good garden,” said Ginger.

“The cutworms are pretty bad yet. I got tired of squishing them, so I saved a bunch for fishing.”

“Where are they?”

“In my pockets.”

“Kitty!”

The younger girl's eyes sparkled. "What fish would eat a cutworm, anyhow? But I did get some earthworms. They are in a bean can at the edge of the garden."

After dinner, Grace and Kitty washed the dishes in a hurry.

When Ginger came from the bedroom, her colorful appearance proclaimed Twyla had convinced at least one sister to "pretty up."

"I thought we were going fishing, not to a pie social," Grace grumbled. "Are you going to put on a dress?"

"Whatever for?"

"Ask them. They caught me this morning and put pins in my snarls before I could get away."

"Poor girl," Kitty teased. "You should have gotten up when I did and went to the garden. If the weather stays as nice as it was before dinner, you won't even have wind to help blow the curls away."

In the ice house, Kitty and Grace each found a clean cotton shirt. Kitty chose a faded sleeveless green plaid, then she tied a lavender scarf around her neck.

"Remember when cousin Dell said you shouldn't wear purple because the color didn't go with your cat eyes?"

"Remember? Sure, I'd like to have shown her right then just how much a cat I am."

"You'd have been hauled out behind the barn for Pop's strap if you had."

"No chance. He's never laid a hand on me, just beats me up with words."

She traded her muddy bibs for a pair of baggy jeans that promptly slid back down in a puddle around her ankles. Grace handed her a length of twine, which when threaded through her belt loops and tied in a square knot, worked just fine.

She picked up a brush. "Want me to do your hair?"

"Not until I get the pins out," Grace answered, ducking away from her sister.

Kitty turned to her own hair and brushed the short, dark mass. When her unruly curls refused to tame, she clamped her old hat down on her head and ran up the ice house steps. At the doorway she came to a sudden stop. The company had arrived.

She hesitated beside the ice house, waiting for Grace to come up the steps. Then the two youngest girls moved into the excitement. After some fuss over poles, lines and bait, part of the group started across the pasture toward the fishing dam.

Frank and Twyla formed the center of the group, flanked by Frank's brother, Brice, and his sister Angel, and her husband Pete, with three small children in tow and a toddler on his father's arm. Ginger walked with the group, which was followed by the two mothers.

Teddy ran ahead of everyone else.

Kitty and Grace remained behind to untangle a drop line for each of them. When the task was done, they wound the drop lines on the foot-long sticks and started after the other fishermen.

"Let's race," Kitty whispered to her companion.

Grace needed no urging, but burst ahead. Kitty was hard put to catch her. They ran with abandon, holding the drop lines well away from their bodies lest they should fall and catch a fishhook in the flesh.

"Those wild girls will never grow up," Ginger uttered when the two sisters raced by the group.

"Couldn't you get them to wear dresses?" asked Twyla.

"I didn't even try," Ginger fell in step beside Brice.

But Angel defended the tomboys. "Well, I'm not wearing a dress. I'd scare the fish." She caught her two-year-old daughter up in her arms and carried her.

"No, but you're not a wild woman like those two."

"Oh? You ought to see me when I get going."

A trickle of laughter ran through the group.

"Hey, I carried that can of worms across the pasture and didn't spill a one," Kitty called to Grace when they reached the fishing dam. Quickly the girls baited their hooks and unrolled the drop lines. They secured the knots holding the cork floats and iron weights.

"I think they should be called swing lines instead of drop lines," Grace remarked, whirling the line round and round above her head. When released from her grip, the line with its float and weight went far out over the water, then settled into place with the float riding the gentle waves caused by a soft breeze.

"Good cast," Kitty exclaimed. She tried several times before her cast pleased her. When the cork was floating far out on the water at last, she plunked herself down at the base of the dam grade. "I'm glad the wind is not blowing hard for once."

"We'll be able to tell when the bobber is dancing with a fish attached and not just riding the waves. Did you bet Ginger you could catch more fish than her?"

"Nope. I wouldn't want to embarrass her in front of Frank's brother."

"His name is Brice, Kitty."

"Ol' Ginger must really be gone on him, huh?"

"Nuts over him," Grace answered.

"Pretty easy for her to be nuts."

"Don't you like her?"

"Sure." Kitty sighed. "I was just trying to be funny. She's okay. She just gets my temper up pretty often."

"Mine, too."

"She told me this morning you were half mad. I'll bet you were all mad, not half. What happened?"

"She got to drive the horses and pull the scraper when we were cleaning the barn. I had to dig the manure loose with a pitchfork. I about swooned in the stink. Every time she'd leave to empty the scraper, I'd stick my head out the window for fresh air. She caught me a couple times and chewed me out. I told her to climb a tree and she came after me. When I told her I'd hit her with the pitchfork handle, she just stood there and sputtered.

"If you and I had been oldest instead of youngest, we would be nice to her, wouldn't we?"

"Nope." Grace smoothed loose dirt with her feet and sat down. "Your float is jumping."

Kitty leaped to her feet, waited until the cork bobber disappeared under the surface of the water, then jerked the line to set the hook in the fish's mouth. Hand over hand she pulled in the line. The first fish of the afternoon was a medium-sized Bullhead.

Angel's oldest little boy came to inspect the fish and asked Kitty. "How come you call da feesh Bullhead?"

"See his horns," the girl indicated the protrusions on the fish's head. With thumb and finger behind the gills, she picked up the Bullhead, which tried to flip back and forth in her grasp. She removed the hook from its mouth and dropped the body into a bucket of water. Before she could cast out her line again, Grace pulled in another Bullhead. Even more fish were grabbing bait and being hauled to shore by persons in the larger group.

As the afternoon wore on, the fishing slowed. Kitty led the older children away from the water and played tag in the grass with them. Teddy left his fishing pole and joined her. When they grew tired of the game, the small ones stretched out to rest on a blanket beside the baby and their mother while Kitty went back to fishing near Grace.

"How many fish have the skirts caught?"

"I don't know. Looks to me like they are intent on catching only one fish apiece."

"And the poor fellows are swallowing the romance hook, line and sinker."

Grace shook her head, "Brice isn't. As for Frank, Twyla stole his heart a long time ago."

Kitty was staring absently into the water when she became aware of someone watching her. She turned her head and met Brice's warm brown eyes. A touch of smile creased his deeply tanned face before he looked back at the water. And this time she knew he was not laughing at her.

Her heart leaped and she muttered, "He'd look good in a sombrero."

"You and your cowboys," Grace replied, not bothering to ask who would look good in a sombrero. "As for me, I'm going to marry a soldier."

"Well, if the United States gets involved in another war, which appears to be coming, there will be plenty of them available. You can catch your soldier before he goes overseas or wait for him to come home."

The fishermen along the dam grade sat nearly motionless while the mid-afternoon sun blazed with intense heat and the fish swam without hurry near the water's surface, ignoring the baited hooks.

Grace went off to count the catch. On her return, she said, "Mom says we have plenty for supper. We'll be leaving soon."

Kitty drew in her line, checked the bait and cast it out again into the water. Brice had stretched out in the sun with his hat over his face. Ginger was watching both lines. Frank and Twyla rolled their lines on poles and sat talking with Pete and Angel.

Later, when the fishing party had returned to the shade on the east side of the house, several of the group prepared to clean the fish. Kitty encouraged Twyla to show Frank the new milk cow's calf, and the couple had gone toward the barn. Ginger went to the house for clean pails while Brice and Pete sharpened knives.

The creaking pump handle added to the noise of chattering fishermen as Ginger brought cold, clear water to the old table near the chicken coop. Brice caught up a Bullhead from the pail of water and the cleaning began.

Angel stood nearby, a sleeping child in her arms. Ginger turned to her, "You can lay the tyke on my bed in the house. I'll show you where." And the young women left.

The others made quick work of cleaning the fish. Heads were removed, bellies slit open and the entrails scraped out.

Grace rinsed the fish as fast as Kitty and Brice cleaned them. She took time to scrub the tails, which would fry up crisp and good, but if not properly scrubbed would carry a muddy taste. "We'll race you guys," she called merrily to the other group.

"Ah, you always want to race at something."

"Well, you know we get things done faster when we race," Grace argued, then lowered her voice for only Brice and Kitty to hear. "Where's your father, Brice?"

"At home. He struck on an idea for a poem this morning. When we left he was still trying to think of a good ending."

"He writes poems? That is so special. We had a teacher once who wrote poetry."

"Yah, Mr. Robinson."

"Where's your dad?" Brice asked in return.

"Pop? Oh, he's around here somewhere. He doesn't think much of anyone loafing around."

"Not even on Sunday?"

"Nope. He's a slave driver."

"Hey, Grace," Kitty warned.

The sisters faced each other, then Grace muttered in the most stubborn voice she could muster, "Well, we do work hard."

"That shows. You have a nice place here."

"Like Ginger says, 'If the good Lord gives you a crop, you'd better hurry and get the grain harvested.' Maybe she's right."

"Even if working on Sundays is included?"

"It seems to."

Brice had not slowed his fish cleaning as he chatted with Grace while Kitty worked silently beside him. Then the young man commented. "We have a neighbor who says the same thing. I heard Dad tell him once that if the Lord gave him a good crop, he ought to at least show his thankfulness by observing Sunday just for the Lord. And my preacher uncle says if the Lord wants you to have a good harvest, He will give you time to get the crop into the granary without working on Sunday." He slid the fish he had just cleaned into the bucket of cold water. "How many left?"

"Not many," Kitty replied to Brice's question. "I like these fish that don't have scales. Scraping off scales would take a lot longer than scrubbing."

"Some folks skin Bullheads, but I figure skinning takes away some of the flavor."

"Sure. Leave the skin and a little mud on. They taste better if you do."

"Awright, you two," Grace pretended to pout. "I'm washing them better than you think. No mud will flavor these fish."

After a moment, she questioned. "Why do we say dress a chicken, but we clean a fish? Why don't we clean a chicken and dress a fish?

"And we dress a deer, but we clean a pheasant?" Brice added.

Before Kitty could add to the conversation, a voice called from the other team. "We beat you guys. You did too much talking."

Kitty shrugged and the three kept working. Grace dumped the water from her dishpan, then started over with clean water from a pail, washing the fish again.

"This is the last one," Kitty said, holding up the wriggling, slippery fish. "Who will have the honor of cleaning him?"

"I will," Brice answered, his large, strong hand closing over both the fish and Kitty's hand.

"L-l-look out. He'll horn you," the girl stammered. She experienced the same warm, good feeling she had felt at the fishing dam when she caught him studying her.

"Why else are they called Bullheads? They have horns like a bull." Grace quizzed, looking hard for a moment at her younger sister's blushing face.

"Well, getting horned is no fun," Kitty found her voice. "You take the fish to the house. I'll clean up here."

The supper was soon ready. Mom had rolled the fish in a mixture of flour, salt and pepper, then fried them in butter. To go with that, there was potato salad, radishes from the garden and glasses of cold milk to drink. Later, there were generous servings of the pies Twyla had labored over the day before.

The table accommodated as many diners as possible. Pop came from the tool shop for a quick supper. He maintained silence at his place, eating without interruption. Kitty, Grace, Pete Brice, and the two oldest children sat on the floor with their plates and cups.

Frank's mother turned to Ginger, "Twyla is coming over to Borders Grove to spend the Fourth of July. Why don't you come, too?"

"Oh yes, do." Twyla encouraged.

"I'd love to," the girl answered.

"You have to milk your cow," Grace teased from her place near Brice and the children.

"Oh, Kitty will milk for me."

"I will?" the sister questioned, her fork of potato salad poised midway between plate and mouth.

"Of course. I'll milk for you tonight and you'll milk for me the night of the picnic."

The subject was dropped without reply. Kitty looked up again and met Brice's warm, brown eyes studying her face. This time his smile spoke understanding. There was no mockery in his expression. She managed to return his smile before he looked away. Then she blushed the deepest rose color ever.

Grace leaned near her and whispered. "Don't ever get red like that in the barn. You'll set the hay afire."

Kitty's face grew even redder.

Small plates of pie slices were passed around and cups refilled. Kitty said she had eaten so many fish she thought she wouldn't need lunch in the pasture for days.

Then the dishes were washed and put away. The fish bones were scraped into the range to be burned so the dog couldn't choke on them. And all too soon, the company got into Frank's car and drove away.

Ginger stood in the barn door when the milking was almost finished. Only Grace and Kitty were left at the chores, the latter stripping the last cow. Grace was waiting at the door of the separator room for Kitty's last pail of milk.

"Nice day, huh?" Grace asked.

"Yes," Ginger replied. "And Brice is so sweet, but he is quiet. He just doesn't talk at all."

Grace met Kitty's eyes across the back of the milk cow, raised her eyebrows, smirked, then turned back to cranking up the separator.

"Kitty, will you let me wear your lavender scarf for the Fourth of July? I'm borrowing Twyla's yellow dress and the scarf would go nicely in my hair."

Kitty paused in the stripping, the milking process which removes the last bit of milk at a setting, "I guess I'll wear the scarf myself."

"What? You'll have to herd the cattle."

"Sure. I thought maybe Bronco would like some purple in his life."

"You're just jealous because you can't go. You're not nice at all."

"And you just destroyed any chance of my changing my mind. I don't think I should have to milk your cows while you go moochin' around the country, or should I say smoochin?"

"Oh, you make me so mad," Ginger whirled away to stomp from the barn.

Kitty pulled the cow's tail to one side, aimed, and used the last squirt of milk to wet the back of her sister's shirt.

Ginger stopped short and wheeled around.

"I reckon you can wear my scarf," Kitty stated. "But next time remember to keep your word about milking for me. You seem to always forget your part of an agreement. I do believe you said you would milk for me tonight. You didn't show up until we were almost finished." She stood up, hung her milking stool on the wall, patted the cow and handed the brimming pail of milk to Grace.

"I had to finish reading an article in my new True Confessions magazine."

"That excuse might work for Teddy, but it won't work for you. Don't even try trading chores with me ever again."

Pop seemed almost happy at supper the next night. "Twyla and I ought to be able to finish cultivating the corn tomorrow. Then let the rain come. The corn will have a good start over the weeds."

"I have a chance to work for the Jonas family again this summer, Pop," Twyla ventured.

"Well, if we get the rain I expect, you'll have plenty to do here. Pass the butter." He spread his thick slice of bread and reached for the Juneberry jam. "I'm going to need you to help fence the pastures. Ginger and I will run into Draper for posts and wire when the cultivating is finished." He turned to the youngest daughter. "How's the grass holding out, Kitty?"

"Okay, but I'm going to move the cattle down the creek about a mile or so."

Pop nodded.

Before they went to bed, Ginger joined the younger girls on the porch. They sat in silence, each with her own thoughts. The frogs by the fishing dam in the pasture were engaged in chorus. Occasionally a Katydid carried out a long solo.

Kitty sighed and murmured, “Fences. My herding days are almost over.”

CHAPTER THREE

Independence Day dawned bright and clear. Before Kitty left with the cattle she tied Bronco to the porch railing and found Twyla and Ginger giggling in their room. Ginger was putting Twyla’s hair in pin curls. She wore Twyla’s yellow dress and Kitty’s lavender scarf was on the dresser, neatly pressed.

“I’m surprised you’re getting all prettied up before breakfast. Pop’s likely to make you do some fencing this morning.”

“Frank is coming for us before ten,” Ginger said around the pins in her mouth. “I’ll tell you about the picnic tonight.”

“I reckon you’ll have lemonade and foot races and fireworks, huh?”

“And lots to eat,” Twyla added. “I wish you and Grace could come, too.”

“Ah, a picnic is just a picnic,” Kitty shrugged and moved away. “Just a lot of people eating a lot of food.” She slipped the reins from the porch railing and swung up on Bronco. The black gelding whirled and loped after the cattle, his sleek black coat glistening as he stretched out. The rush of wind from his running dried Kitty’s tears before they had a chance to streak her cheeks.

The day was slightly cooler than the preceding ones had been. Still, the heat pressed in closely around Kitty. Bronco went down to the creek and stood in the water while Kitty went wading. Today she did not lie in the shade and dream of her cowboy. She kept her eyes wide open to keep away the face which had come to her so often in the past two weeks. If she closed her eyes, she saw the wavy, dark hair and warm brown eyes and his endearing smile. And today she did not want to picture him at the picnic with her sisters.

Kitty was glad when the day ended. She tarried long with the cattle as darkness came. She was near home when Bronco shied suddenly. A flash caught her attention and she searched the western skyline until she saw a white streak and a burst of faint stars.

She hurried the cattle into the lot, closed the gate and called Grace from the house.

The girls rode double on Bronco to the top of a nearby hill. Then they sat together and watched the faraway fireworks until the last burst died away.

"Guess the picnic has ended," Kitty mused, rising from her place and stretching.

"I bet Pop works those girls mighty fiercely tomorrow."

"Maybe. They'll probably be home in an hour or two. Ginger said she'd come tell us all about the day. Let's get down to bed and catch forty winks before she gets here. I should have brought the cattle in earlier, but it was too stinking hot to move them until after dark. Did Teddy actually help you with the milking?"

"Yes. So did Mom."

"Well, having to help with chores is good for Teddy, but Mom shouldn't have to help out when I don't get home in time."

They undressed and were lying in restless silence when Ginger crept down the ice house stairway. Kitty rolled over, sat up and groped for the lantern and matches.

"Don't make a light. We don't want the folks to see I'm over here. I think Pop's mad."

"How come you think that?"

"The door was locked. You know we never lock the door. I think he wanted to make us get him out of bed so he could chew us out good. Twyla climbed in our bedroom window and I came over here."

Grace giggled in the darkness. "Anyway, did you have fun?"

"Oh yes. You girls ought to have seen the races. The men raced their teams against each other, pulling loaded hayracks across the pasture. Brice was driving a pair of young chestnut geldings. They shone like fire in the sun, and he was driving them like Atlas."

"Now you sound like you have been reading too many Zane Grey novels."

"Oh, but he was so strong and handled the horses so well."

"Were they his father's horses?"

"No. Brice works on the Williams Ranch. I heard his mother say so. He broke those horses himself, though."

"Well, of course," Grace said. "Did you have lots to eat?"

"I sure did."

"Has Frank left yet?"

"Yes, he left right away. I think Twyla wanted him to go before Pop came out with the shotgun or something."

"You really think he's mad, huh?"

"I'm afraid so. I'd better get to the house now. I'll have to sneak in the window like Twyla did."

The next morning Kitty was surprised to find the usually empty kitchen full of family preparing for breakfast. She sensed there was trouble lurking at Pop's place as Ginger set the table. Twyla was silently frying eggs and bacon while Mom deftly toasted bread over the flame in the range.

"Where's Grace?" Pop growled.

"Still asleep."

"Well, go get her. There will be no lying in bed today. We'll set a mile of fence by sunup."

Kitty ran back through the wet grass to the ice house and hollered down the stairs. "Hey, bail out and come take your punishment."

"What did I do?" Grace grumbled sleepily.

"Nothing. Just hurry up and you can enjoy the prettiest part of the day. But put on your protective turtle shell or someone is likely to spoil every hour for you."

When Grace came sleepily to the table, the family sat down. Ginger repeated the prayer, then they began to eat. Only Pop looked at Twyla without picking up his fork.

"How long have you been seeing this Frank fellow?"

Twyla's bite of bacon hesitated between her plate and mouth, then slowly her hand lowered and she raised her eyes to meet those of her stepfather. "I started running around with him last summer when I worked for the Jonas family."

"Sneaking around that long? Well, I don't want to ever see him around here again."

"He's coming over Sunday."

"No, he's not," Pop retorted. "Write him a letter or something, but I don't want to see him hanging around keeping you from your work and giving you foolish ideas. On second thought, do not write a letter. I'll meet him at the door when he shows up. He will get the message that he is not welcome around here. Now get to work."

"Work is all you think of," Twyla blazed. "Well, I'll build your fence from here to the H Bar H, but don't go interfering in my personal life. I haven't been sneaking around and if I have foolish ideas, they have come because you have tried to drive my dreams away since the day you took over this family." The oldest sister leaped to her feet and started for the door.

"Twyla," Ginger chided, "you've hurt Pop's feelings."

When Twyla hesitated, Grace swallowed the last of her egg. "Other folks have feelings, too," she stated. "Wait up, Twyla. I'll help you with the fence."

"You forgot your turtle shell," Kitty thought.

The screen door banged and the remaining family members were left in a strained silence.

"Do you need me to stay home and help with the fence today?" Kitty quizzed.

"No," he growled in return. "We've got to save the grass in the home pastures if at all possible. Take the cattle out."

She finished her breakfast as calmly as possible and then made her exit.

The cattle moved readily out of the lot when she opened the gate. Then she caught Bronco, climbed on his back and rode to where Twyla and Grace were already busy digging a post hole. "I've got an idea, Twyla."

The oldest sister looked up at the youngest, masking any traces of feeling.

"Write a note to Frank and I'll mail the envelope from the box at the old schoolhouse. If I put the flag up, the mailman will stop and pick up the letter. You figure out a way to go with me Sunday when I take the herd out. You can meet Frank at the schoolhouse. Pop didn't say you couldn't see him again. He just doesn't want him here."

"You know what he meant, though. Just because he accused me of sneaking around isn't any reason to do so."

"Hey, this is exciting," Grace added. "Don't let Pop stand in the way of love."

"What do you know about love?" Twyla queried.

"I know I'd like some."

Kitty turned Bronco and rode after the departing cattle.

When Pop and Ginger came out to string wire, Twyla waited for an opportunity, then with her sisters as witnesses, she openly apologized to the little man. "I'm sorry I spoke harshly. I ask you to forgive me. I'll try to do better with controlling my temper."

Pop shrugged. "We all have to blast off once in a while."

During the following week the older girls worked on the fence. Twyla drove her younger sisters until they grumbled, but she was relentless at driving herself. Every morning before sunrise, when Kitty was turning out the cattle, she saw the other girls already at work, digging post holes, setting and tamping posts and stringing barbed wire. Often the pounding of staples being driven to hold the wire in place rang in Kitty's ears when she came home at dusk. Even Teddy had a part in building the fence, running errands, bringing fresh water to the other workers and even pounding staples into posts.

Sunday morning Twyla was absent from the breakfast table. When she did not respond to the girls' bids, Pop went to the bedroom door, "Come on. We've got to finish the fence and get started with the haying before the grass dries up."

"Oh, let her rest a day," urged Mom. "She's had a hard week."

"We've got to finish the fence."

"Then I'll come help," Mom replied, reaching behind her to loosen her apron strings.

Grace started to protest, but her mother's expression warned her to keep quiet.

Grumbling under his breath, Pop sat down to his breakfast.

"I feel so cheap," Twyla said later when was riding behind Kitty on Bronco. "Now Mom has gone out to help build the fence."

"Well, she enjoys doing something different for a change. Like herding cattle is for me, I suppose housework and gardening and feeding the chickens gets to be a drab routine after so many years. I just hope Pop has sense enough not to push her too hard."

"He won't. She'll push herself. Mom wouldn't know what to do if there came a day when she couldn't work from dawn until dark."

Kitty appreciated Twyla's company. The hours of the morning passed by until the girls ate their sandwiches beside the creek, then Twyla climbed on Bronco and rode to the schoolhouse to meet Frank.

The prairie gaped in lonely silence for Kitty after her sister had gone. She slept in the shade of a tree. Later, she wandered off in search of a last faded Bluebell to take home to Grace, but found none. The cattle were idle, lying in the hot sun, their sides heaving in the afternoon heat.

Sunset was fading when Twyla returned, but the heat held steady and Bronco was sweating, the lather on his neck foaming against the leather bridle reins. Twyla slid off and handed Kitty a book.

"Frank brought this for you from his father's collection."

Kitty stroked the treasure with eager fingers. "But what if Pop sees a new book? He will know your secret."

"He won't pay any attention. Anyway, there is no name showing identification."

"But I couldn't lie if he asked where the book came from. After my mess-up with Ginger's book, he will be suspicious. I'll just have to manage to keep this out of sight. Thanks so much, Sis."

"Wait to thank Frank. The book for you was his idea."

"Well, his idea will make a few hot days go by much faster. Let's start home now. These old girls won't be much of a mind to travel."

"The temp should cool down soon. We seldom get many hot nights in early July."

"If we do, I think I'll start sleeping out here instead of driving the cattle back and forth."

After supper and dish washing, the girls walked to the fishing dam and chased the summer's heat with a swim in the cool water. Stripped down to their bib overalls, they splashed each other and silenced the frog chorus with shrieks and laughter. And later they slept away the night without stirring.

July wore on with endless heat and no rain. The fence around one pasture had long been completed and the haying begun. Kitty saw her days of herding slip away as the first section of fence was finished. By next summer, there would be little need for daily attention to the cattle from Bronco and herself.

Pop's team, Bert and Dick, earned their keep during the haying season. First they pulled the mower to cut down the grass, then they were employed to pull the rake to gather the hay into long windrows. Finally, the sun-dried grass was pitched on a rack and the faithful team pulled the load to the barn where the hay was rolled up into the loft. If rain provided an abundant crop of hay in a summer season, what would not fit in the barn loft was carefully stacked in a fenced yard some distance from the buildings.

"We sure could use another team," Pop remarked one evening. "This haying would go a lot faster."

"Looks to me like we are about done haying for this year unless we get some rain," Ginger suggested.

Pop scowled. "We'll do good to fill the loft, let alone make any stacks elsewhere. I sure don't like the weather. Makes a farmer nervous to have things so dry again after just coming through years of dust storms and starvation."

Kitty was well supplied with reading material as Twyla and Frank continued to meet at the schoolhouse. Sometimes Twyla went at night and Kitty thought of the morning when she might find Bronco and her sister still missing. She was sure some day Twyla would go with Frank and not come back.

When the haying was finished, there were hot days when the family relaxed around the house. Even Pop settled into his chair and tried to rest in the hottest hours of midday. Grace and Ginger retired to the cool depths of the ice house bedroom and pretended to feel sorry for Kitty out under the hot sun.

"She gets out of a gob of work out there sleeping under the sun."

"Have you ever tried her job? You'd go stark raving mad without someone to pick on," Grace retorted.

Mom brought her churning and sat with the girls in the ice house. She had filled the glass jar half full of cream, added a touch of butter coloring, screwed on the lid, and now her nimble arm was making the paddle fly around, whipping the cream.

"Butter coloring at this time of year?" Grace questioned.

"Surprising, yes, but the other day my butter was so pale. I think the milk cows just aren't getting enough green grass. I'm sorry they can't go out with the range cows and get something better to eat."

"We'd never get the evening milking done if we had to wait for Kitty to bring in the milk cows."

"Here, let me turn the crank awhile for you."

"Thank you. My arm is getting tired."

Mom settled back in the chair while Ginger churned. Soon the cream in the jar began to grain and separate from the buttermilk.

Grace climbed lazily off the bed. "I'll go work the butter."

Back in the hot kitchen, she poured the buttermilk off the bright yellow lump, then with a wooden paddle, she worked the grains of butter in Mom's big bowl until she could no longer squeeze out any more buttermilk. Then the finished product was salted and packed in Mom's butter mold, which would make a pound block. After the butter hardened in the ice box, it was eased out of the mold, wrapped in waxed paper and carried to the cellar to be stored until needed or sold.

Ginger came to the house with ice slivers she had chipped off a block in the old ice house. She floated them in a tall glass of buttermilk and carried the drink to Pop. Grace covered the rest of the buttermilk with a clean towel for storage. Buttermilk was a basic ingredient in Mom's cakes and morning pancakes.

On a Sunday afternoon, Twyla appeared on Pop's horse. She was passing up the creek to meet Frank, but had made an excuse of bringing Kitty a cold container of iced water. "Drink slowly or you'll get sick."

Kitty laid aside her book. "I'll drink slowly to make the pleasure last longer. The water in my canteen is about hot enough to scald a chicken for picking." Kitty watched her sister nervously slapping at her leg with the bridle reins. "What's bugging you?"

"I'm afraid Pop is suspicious or maybe even knows what I'm doing."

"So? He just said he didn't want to see Frank around the place. He didn't say you couldn't ever see him again."

"Just the same, he's going to have his say again, and soon, I think."

"Well, much as I like your company, I wouldn't stand around here worrying if I had a good-looking young man waiting with open arms for me."

Kitty watched as Twyla took her advice and moved off in the direction of the schoolhouse. She wondered if this might be the day the girl would not return. She pictured Pop's horse arriving home without a rider, with the reins knotted in the bridle. She could imagine the panic of the family and the efforts of Pop to stop something inevitable.

She turned back to her book. This was one of poetry, something with which she was not very familiar. She had been sure she wouldn't like reading poetry, however, the musical lyrics soon caught her up in a rollicking cowhand's song or a lover's farewell to her dying man.

The house was ablaze with lamplight when Kitty returned. Of late she had arrived home when the moon was high and her world a silent sleeping one. Her mother would be alone in the kitchen with a single lamp burning low, waiting for her youngest daughter.

Tonight Kitty was met by Grace at the lot. When the last cow and Bronco came in, Grace shut the gate behind them. Kitty slid off and slipped the bridle from Bronco's head.

"What's loose?" She nodded toward the house.

"Aunt and Uncle are here from Montana," Grace hopped from one foot to the other. "They saw Pop's horse and Frank's at the school house and very innocently asked Pop what anyone would be doing there at this season of the year. Later Twyla rode in and Pop asked, 'Is this the horse you saw?' I guess Twyla will catch the devil now."

A chill crept down over Kitty. Even though her step-father had never laid a hand on any of the girls, she was nervous about the emotional abuse he was capable of handing out.

The cattle grazed in the newly-fenced pasture the next day. The family fished and Mom talked of old things and past times with her brother and his wife.

Twyla cooked milk, sugar and eggs to make a thick custard. Then she added vanilla and cream and poured the mixture into the ice cream can before setting the cap in place. Kitty and Grace chipped pieces of ice and packed the freezer, alternating ice with handfuls of coarse salt. Then they cranked the handle and the freezer can went around and around in the middle of the ice. Finally, the crank turned with some difficulty, signaling the hardness of the frozen custard. Kitty wiped ice and salt from the lid of the can and Grace lifted the container from the salty ice water bath. Then they hurried into the house with the can.

Twyla scooped the rich ice cream into big bowls. She put the dasher on a platter for Kitty to clean with a small spoon.

Even Pop came from repairing the cultivator to share the ice cream.

Late in the afternoon, as the guests were preparing to leave, Kitty found Twyla in her room, carefully packing her things into a pasteboard box.

"Whatever are you doing?"

"I guess I'm going to Montana," she did not try to hide her tears.

"Maybe you'll have fun," Grace attempted to encourage her sister from where she sat on the big bed.

Kitty was aghast. "Why ever would Pop send his best hired man so far away?"

A touch of smile twinkled from the oldest sister, "I guess he hopes I'll forget Frank."

"You can't blame him really, Twyla," Ginger ventured. "Pop has done a lot for us. The least we can do is help him build this ranch into something big like he wants."

Kitty tried to bite back a surge of anger, but words spilled. "This ranch was already big when he took ownership, and don't forget the only reason he got it was because it was part of the package, which came with our widowed mother and four daughters who have worked night and day to please him." Kitty took the lavender scarf from her own neck and tied it around Twyla's. "I for one wish I was going with you."

"You didn't get the fence built to the H Bar H Ranch," Grace made a weak stab at a joke.

"Well, the fence is your worry, now," Twyla replied, then her eyes blazed. "My working days on this place are over." She folded the flaps shut on the box and tied knots in the binder twine wraps in a final gesture.

She made one last appeal to Pop, "I was supposed to meet Frank Saturday evening. Would you send one of the girls to tell him I've gone away?"

"Don't worry. He'll soon catch on to something when you don't come to meet him. He'll get the idea. You don't need him around."

Just before Twyla climbed into the car, Kitty leaned close to her sister in a hug. "Don't worry, sis," she whispered. "I'll let him know."

The automobile jerked, roared and rolled away midst shouts of farewell. Mom's shoulders shook visibly while Kitty hurried away to the barn to cry alone.

Later, in the shelter of the ice house, she took pen and paper and wrote Frank. "With regret I must tell you Twyla will not be able to meet you Saturday evening. They done packed her off to no man's land, baggage and all. I have no idea when she will escape and come running home to you. Never fear the waning of her love, which will not fade. No man could take your place in her life. I wish I might have come to meet you and told you this in person, but I fear the sentry will be on duty that evening."

After she sealed the envelope she reviewed the words mentally. What if...what if the sister's love did wax cold among the handsome young men in the Big Sky Country? She brushed the thought away, knowing her oldest sister too well. She was convinced the love between Frank and Twyla would only grow stronger each day they were apart..

Mom agreed with Kitty's thoughts during their private breakfast the next morning. She slipped Kitty a postage stamp as she said, "Absence makes the heart grow fonder, they say." She drew Kitty's lavender scarf from her pocket and tied it around the girl's neck. "Twyla asked me to return this and remember how much she loves you."

Kitty carried the letter in a pocket of her bib behind her sandwiches. She left the cattle grazing a few miles from home and made a hurried trip down the road to mail the note from her cousin Dell's mailbox.

CHAPTER FOUR

Late Saturday afternoon a horse and rider appeared on the horizon. Kitty lowered her book and watched uncertainly until she clearly made out the markings of Pop's horse. She slipped the book inside the bib of her overalls, glanced about to be sure the cattle had not strayed too far, then relaxed against the trunk of the tree.

"Hi, lazybones." Ginger called out with a merry voice.

"Lo," Kitty answered with suspicion, wondering, "Whatever is she doing out here?"

Ginger slid off the bare back of the horse and hobbled his front feet. Then she flopped down beside Kitty.

"Looks like you plan to stay awhile."

"Uh-huh. I thought you might like some company on this stuffy, hot day."

Kitty broke off a piece of grass, slit the dry cover from the stem with her thumbnail and chewed the soft, sweet center. "Misery loves company, or something like that."

"You don't seem very enthused about my presence."

Kitty shrugged, thinking "Not when I know you are up to no good," but saying, "I'm just not used to unexpected visitors." She grinned, "You didn't even give me time to sweep the floor or bake a cake."

"Sorry 'bout that. The telegraph line was down between my house and yours."

"H-m-m," Kitty drew forth her book. "Just let me finish my chapter and then we'll go see if we can find a coyote den. I have suspicions where there is one."

"Coyote den? You carry a gun?"

"You know I don't. And I wouldn't shoot baby coyotes if I did have a gun."

"A coyote is a coyote."

"You ought to know."

"What's that supposed to mean?"

"They sneak around and do their dirty work, regardless of how old they are. Now you know what I mean?"

For some unknown reason Ginger did not answer her sister. Instead, she let her read a few minutes, then interrupted, "Where did you get your book?"

"Frank."

"He was here already?"

Kitty scowled. "No. He's never been here."

Ginger hesitated, sorting her thoughts. "Books from Frank, sort of a bribe to keep your mouth shut about the meetings at the schoolhouse, huh?"

Kitty lowered the book and her green eyes glared at Ginger. "I wouldn't have to be bribed to keep my mouth shut, unlike some people I know. The loan of books was a favor on Frank's part."

Ginger ignored the sarcasm, "How are you going to return them?"

Kitty shrugged. "Mail, I suppose, unless you want to interfere. Pop would probably give you a ride over there the next time you go to town, just for being his faithful little spy. Then you could see Brice."

The older sister glowered. "Mailing is your only option. But, of course, you could keep them for the rest of your life as a sort of souvenir."

"Oh, you are so funny. See me laughing?"

They did not find the coyote den. The hours of the hot afternoon drug by with Kitty making an effort to avoid any further quarrel. The day's dullness was broken temporarily when the milk cow's yearling steer charged toward them. Ginger jumped up while Kitty appeared to ignore the critter. With his tail held straight out behind him like a broom handle, the steer plunged over the creek bank and splashed into the stagnant water.

"Heel flies," Kitty said as Ginger's fear-weakened legs dropped her back to sit on the ground. "Haven't you ever seen anything with heel flies?"

"No," Ginger snorted. "I don't live with these critters like you do. You might be part cow, but you can't expect me to sit still when a crazy steer practically runs over me."

"Being part cow is sure better than being part coyote," Kitty muttered, then gushed, "there, there, my dear, you are safe now. Just trust me to take care of you out on this wild prairie."

"You talk about me reading mush magazines! You sound like something out of a Zane Grey novel."

"H-m-m. I don't know how you would know what is in a Zane Grey book. But, I do wish I had one to read right now."

"You spend entirely too much time lazing away the hours out here with books. I think the time has come for someone else to take over the cattle herding and you learn how to do some real work."

"Good luck, podner," Kitty replied, and returned to her reading. She made no further attempt to even converse with the intruder.

They lingered into the twilight hours, allowing the cattle to graze, then pushed the herd slowly home. Because of the heat and concern for Bronco, Kitty walked to give her horse a break. She didn't bother trying to convince Ginger to give her mount the same privilege. She was thankful for enough daylight to avoid stepping on cactus or snakes. The cattle were safely in the home lot before night dropped a cover of black over the prairie.

She was surprised to find Pop sitting on the house step in the darkness. The hour was long past his usual bedtime. "Too hot to sleep?" she asked in mock innocence. He grunted in return.

"You go on in, Kitty," Ginger said and lingered behind to speak quietly to Pop.

Kitty obeyed and went into the house, but her ears burned as she realized the spy was reporting to the boss man. She went back to the doorway and the voices outside stilled. "Where is Mom?"

"I sent her to bed. You're a big girl, now. You can find your own supper."

No longer feeling hungry, Kitty stepped out on the porch and slipped over the side, avoiding the step, "Don't forget to put away the food and wash your dishes, Ginger."

"Getting kind of bossy, aren't you? You sure ate in a hurry."

"All of a sudden I wasn't hungry." Kitty fled to the ice house before her anger boiled over into public space.

She let the ice house door slam behind her and flounced down the stairs. Grace stirred in the bed. "What's going on?"

"What's going on?" Grace repeated in a voice masked by sleepiness.

"Why's Pop sitting outside at this hour?"

"Oh," the smaller girl stretched. "Twyla was supposed to meet Frank tonight, remember? Well now, which one of Twyla's little sisters might sneak off to tell Frank where his sweetheart went?"

Kitty slumped down on the bed. "Figures. Ginger spent all afternoon in the pasture with me. I'd like to have seen her stop me if I had been going to go to the schoolhouse." She sat up straight and grabbed her hair brush, stroking the brown tresses until sparks flew in the darkness. "And Pop has been standing guard over you?"

"And over the place. Frank couldn't sneak in if he was Ol' Slewfoot himself."

Kitty chuckled, slicked off her shirt and overalls and rolled into bed, "Is he going to sit out there all night?"

"Hardly. He'll wait until he figures Frank has given up and gone home. Then he'll go to his bed and sleep like a just-fed puppy."

"Well, I'm going to be snoring before he even finds his bed," Kitty answered, snuggling her head in the fluff of her pillow.

After a minute Grace's voice came through the darkness, "Don't you feel sorry for Frank?"

"Nope," and she was asleep.

CHAPTER FIVE

And still the heat of July burned on. The evening after Kitty spent a night out on the range, she fashioned a pack to use for a pillow and lunch bag. With heavy string from the shoe repair kit she sewed across the bottom of a thirty-inch length of canvas pant leg she had swiped from the rag bag. She cut holes near the top of the bag and ran an old scarf through them, which could be pulled up and tied to hold her canteen and some odds and ends of food. The bag was tied on behind the cantle of the saddle, her use of which, incidentally, no one argued over any longer. The problem with riding a saddle, though, was that she had to wear her bulky old winter lace-up shoes and socks besides. The shoes helped prevent getting a leg hung up in a stirrup in case of accident. And the socks prevented blisters from the shoes when she walked.

In the days that followed, her sparse diet peeled away any excess pounds she had carried over from childhood while the sun bronzed her complexion and bleached her hair.

If she could find a tree or a shaded creek bank, she often slept there during most of the afternoon and early evening. Night time brought little relief from the heat, but at least the relentless sun rested a while. When the moon gave enough light to move about safely, she led Bronco in circles around the herd just for something to do. She rested often, giving her horse opportunity to find scant patches of grass to eat. By sleeping in the heat of the day she had little concern for rattlesnakes or rabid skunks. She knew for a fact the reptiles would not be out in the intense heat. Rabid skunks were a whole different worry; one she had to trust God to handle.

Often she left the cattle in search of a new waterhole in the creek that might give some relief to the thirsty critters. She hoped even to find a spring-fed basin that might be free of moss and tumbleweeds.

It was on such a search in the early morning light that she rode along the top of the creek bank, paying more intent for a glimpse of water than the terrain. Without warning, the ground crumbled under Bronco's hooves.

He tumbled head over heels down the embankment, pitching his rider to the side on the way down to the creek bed. Kitty sailed into space, then crashed and slid in the shale and rocks toward the bottom. When the dust cleared, the girl lay very still.

Bronco scrambled to his feet, shook himself and crept cautiously near his mistress. Then he whinnied.

Kitty's hand raised slightly and fell back as she gasped for breath. After a while she rolled over, then sat up. Finally she rose on trembling legs, leaned against her patient horse and patted him. “Guess we took a little spill there, old boy. I sure enough got the wind knocked clean out of me and my left ankle is on fire. I'm guessing you might have a sore spot of two of your own.”

She unbuckled the cinch and pulled off the battered saddle. The sweat-soaked saddle blanket followed. She ran careful hands over Bronco's back, then up and down his neck. Limping around to the other side, she checked him for damage. He did not flinch. If he was hurting, he wasn't showing it.

When her inspection was finished, she replaced the blanket and saddle, put her uninjured foot in the stirrup on the wrong side of the horse and pulled herself up.

She now had no choice. The cattle had to be driven slowly to the artesian well on the H Bar H ranch. The sun would be hot and scorching by the time they reached water. Kitty touched heels to the horse and they made their way with caution as they gathered the cows and calves and pointed them northwest. She prayed no H Bar H cowboys would choose that afternoon to check the well.

She went home late that afternoon. With sides heaving, the cattle made fair time as soon as they realized where they were going. Back in the home lot, they rushed to the dam and gulped the tepid water.

In the house at last, Kitty settled gratefully on a kitchen chair while her mother prepared hot water and Epsom salts in a deep old dishpan. She insisted Kitty soak the injured ankle, and the girl put the other foot in the pan, too, relieved as the hot water softened callouses and soaked away layers of dirt.

Pop inspected her ankle. "Looks like we'll have to cut it off," he teased. Kitty recalled the time when as a little girl she had stuck her foot in a quart jar and couldn't get it out until he threatened to cut it off.

But then the little man stated seriously, "You look all washed out, Kitty. Maybe you'd better stick around the ice house for a day or two and rest. Ginger can take the cattle out to pasture."

"In this heat?" the older girl argued. "And who is going to help Mom if I take Kitty's place. Neither of these two tomboys knows how to cook."

"Oh, I'll manage," Mom said, "I always do."

Ginger's helpless plea moved from Mom to Pop, and over their heads she caught Kitty's mocking silent "Ha, ha, ha."

But in the morning she stuffed her pack with food and a canteen of water to last her until she would be forced to share whatever water the cattle found. On the way to the barn she gritted her teeth and tried to hide the pain shooting up her leg as she limped across the yard.

She climbed up on the corral fence upon seeing Ginger had bridled Pop's horse. When her sister brought the horse near the fence, Kitty slipped on to his back, muttered a "thank you" and followed the cattle out of the corral and back west across the prairie.

Bronco protested being left behind for a rest. The black horse paced up and down the fence, whinnying as the cattle departed. Then he stood at the gate, watching until the last straggler was out of sight.

With the arrival of a full moon, Kitty again rode in the coolness of night as the cattle grazed. Like the cattle, she slept during the day, for hours at a time. She no longer entertained daydreams, but lay in a silent blackness, waiting for she knew not what. The cattle lay panting under the hot July sun, or stood with listless, drooping heads.

One evening she awoke to find the appearance of a sunset in the eastern sky. She thought perhaps she had lost her sense of direction as she watched leaping pink cover the usual blue. Or perhaps she had slept all day and then all night and it was actually sunrise. Finally she noted the faint orange and red horizon was only a topping for billowing clouds of thick smoke. A prairie fire was raging in the east.

For a night and a day Kitty watched the flames advance westward, consuming dried grasses, weeds and any other flammable thing that couldn't be moved.

Toward evening, Grace appeared, riding Bronco. “We’ve plowed a strip from north to south,” she informed Kitty. “But who knows if the plowing will stop the fire. Pop is ready to build a backfire if we must. Jonases lost all their hay and buildings in the flames yesterday. I guess the fire started just east of them.”

“I’m hoping the wind forgets to blow yet a while,” Kitty replied. “Can the fire be brought under control, you think?”

“Maybe. There are cowhands from the H Bar H helping and other men from all around the country. Yesterday I saw Brice go by with some other fellows from the Williams Ranch. He had those beautiful chestnut geldings hitched to a wagon hauling a tank of water. After a while they came back and filled the tank at our fishing dam. Pop didn’t say a word, but you could tell it hurt to let any of his water go.”

Kitty shrugged, “The water won’t do him much good if he loses everything else in the fire.”

“I brought you some grub. Mom said I should bring your rain slicker, but I didn’t.”

“My rain slicker,” Kitty echoed. “What in the world for?”

“Which is what I asked Mom and she said, 'Folks are praying, dear.’ She didn't say anything more. Didn’t try to explain what she meant or nothing.”

Kitty hesitated before answering. “Well, if she thinks it is going to rain, it is going to rain.”

“You have a lot of faith in Mom.”

“I have a lot of faith in Mom’s faith. If Pop had the same kind of faith our mother has, we’d be a lot happier family.”

“Ah, he has religion of a sort.”

“But he doesn’t know how to give himself to Jesus Christ and look for God’s will in his life.”

Grace’s mouth gaped. “You have been reading too much. What kind of silly talk is this?”

Only what your mother has attempted to teach you every minute since you were born, Grace. However, she doesn't teach in words. The life she lives reflects an inner peace with her Maker. Somewhere along the line, Mom felt the need to make Jesus number one in her life. No, she doesn't preach, you can just tell she's different by the things she does."

"And how about you?"

"What about me?"

"You've felt this need, too?"

"Yes," she considered her answer. "There was this book I read at school a long time ago. And little bits I've read from Mom's Bible. Out here under God's great blue sky, the little bits and pieces started falling together and I said," she hesitated, "I said something like this, 'Well God, you know me better than I know me, but I reckon if by dying on the cross Jesus could make eternal life for me, then I want to know your son Jesus Christ, and I'd like a little slice of the eternal life you promised.'"

"What a mouthful. Still, I don't see you acting much like Mom."

Kitty faced her older sister, "I know. And I also know I will probably never begin to reach the peace and gentleness my mother has."

Grace sighed.

Kitty crumbed a dry clod between her hands and let the dust trickle through her fingers. Her eyes had watched the eastern sky until she could see the fire line without looking. "The cattle have sensed the fire and are beginning to get restless. I'll be moving them on west tonight."

"How far west?"

"I don't know," Kitty replied. "I'm hoping to find another well so the herd will have water. You take Pop's horse home and leave Bronco with me. I'll see you in a week or so."

"Do you have enough food?"

"I'll manage."

"Sure you will," Grace stuttered in amazed anger as she emptied Kitty's pack of a book, half of what might once have been an apple and a small piece of dry bread. "What would you have eaten if our mother's insight hadn't told her to send food to you?"

Kitty shrugged wearily, "I don't get very hungry. Take the book, too, I've finished the reading."

"Lucky for you, because when I get done with your pack, there won't be room for any book." Grace untied the flour sack from behind her saddle and moved its contents into Kitty's duffel. First she put in several hard-boiled eggs with intact shells, then apples and wrapped slices of bread and butter. Handing a large piece of chocolate cake to Kitty, she commented, "Mom had just taken this out of the oven when I left. You are to eat it now, all of it."

When Kitty tried to share the sweet, Grace demurred. "I had a piece at home. I am leaving now so I can get home before dark. You take care of yourself."

Kitty watched her sister ride away. When she disappeared from sight, the prairie loomed too big and too quiet. She ate the chocolate cake bit by bit, catching every crumb and letting the flavor last on her tongue. Then she peeled an egg and ate it.

The cattle stayed all that night near the well on the H Bar H Ranch. At dawn, Kitty and Bronco pushed the herd north to a large creek along which banks the trail led, with Kitty searching for signs of a waterhole or cattle trails leading to a dam on one of the large draws.

At midday only an occasional curl of smoke rose in the east, convincing Kitty the prairie fire was under control. She breathed a sigh of relief and a prayer of thanksgiving. She peeled and ate another egg, wondering how long they would keep in the heat of the day and if she could tell by looking at them if they were spoiled, and if she would get sick if she ate a moldy egg. Or do boiled eggs mold or get rotten.

The cattle drank at a stagnant pool of water in the creek, then wandered about, nibbling at an occasional spear of green grass. Bronco picked his way with care, lest he stub a hoof in a large crack and spill his rider.

Kitty saw the milk cow's steer start up a shallow draw as if he was being chased. "You always have to be difficult," she scolded. She started Bronco after him, but the steer plunged on at a fast pace and disappeared over a rise of ground.

Kitty found him a few minutes later, standing belly deep in a pond of water. A few outlying draws were green with spring fed grass. Kitty wheeled Bronco to go back for the cattle and met them coming to her. Like the steer, they had picked up the scent of water. She ate the last boiled eggs.

She lost count of the days they spent at the dam. In the burning heat of the day, the cattle stood in the water, coming out to graze at night. Even as the green grass disappeared Kitty lived with the fear of someone coming to drive them away from the watering hole.

She stripped the saddle and blanket off Bronco as well as her shoes and socks. The latter went in the bag that had once been stuffed with food.

When the enduring heat threatened her sanity, she busied her mind, reviewing multiple facts she had learned in school, reciting all the poetry she could remember, naming states and birds and flowers, and at last, writing a novel in her mind.

She thought about going swimming in the watering hole, but she decided that wouldn't be a smart idea, so she sat at the edge with her feet in the water.

And she prayed; not eloquent speeches, but rather innocent pleas like those of a child's heart.

At last a day came when the sky grew heavy with clouds. The beasts as well as the girl were thankful for the break in the heat. Kitty kept busy throughout the cooler day exploring the pastureland surrounding the dam. She tried to calculate how long the grass in the area would feed the cattle. How long the crumbs in her pack would feed her was a problem she did not want to think about. She even contemplated roping a cow and stealing some milk. She figured by the time she was that hungry, she would be too weak to catch the cow.

The next day brought even heavier clouds. She shivered in spite of herself and wondered how heat could disappear so fast. She dug her shirt from the bag behind her saddle and buttoned it on right over her bib. After rolling the sleeves to the elbow, she reluctantly dug the shoes and socks out and put them on. Then she set about saddling her horse.

The rain started with a soft drizzle, spatting on the ground and making ragged splotches in the dust on Kitty's hands and forearms. After a few minutes, the drizzle increased in volume and force.

She mounted and started the herd toward home, but had only moved a short distance when the wind struck. As the storm rose to a howl, driving rain, the cattle turned tail and drifted back towards Kitty.

The girl's shiver was violent. How she wished Grace had obeyed their mother and brought the rain slicker. There was no available shelter to her knowledge and she knew the storm could last for hours. She considered leaving the herd and facing Bronco into the driving rain, but the idea was given no opportunity to grow. The vision of Pop's accusing face stopped the thought. No way could she stand against his wrath if she showed up at home without the cattle.

Hunched over the horse, Kitty let the rain beat on her back, feeling the wetness trickle down her legs and drip off her old shoes. Bronco began to drift with the herd. The girl lost consciousness of time and feeling. She felt the need to get off and walk beside the horse, but she didn't move from her place. When her stomach growled for food, she ignored the feeling.

The rain slicked her clothes down wet and cold against her skin and plastered her hair against her head.

An hour or so later, the storm stopped as suddenly as it had begun. The late afternoon sun glared with golden brilliance across the rain-drenched prairie as clouds scudded to get out of the way. Bronco and his rider were renewed by the change in weather and the horse moved with quick steps to turn the cattle and push them toward home.

Kitty clung with a nervous grip to Bronco's mane when he followed the cattle as they plunged through rushing creek streams. The flailing rain had packed the ground and ran off in tiny streams which were building into torrents.

Across the miles a little dark-haired mother stood before the screen door, her eyes searching the nighttime darkness. Her sturdy arms rested across her waist. Darkness had blotted out the day many hours before and the rest of the family were sleeping. Still, she stood again at the door. She could not guess how many times she had come to peer out into the darkness after the family went to bed. A light breeze swept across the rain-drenched earth and breathed sweetness on her face. Inhaling deeply of its exhilarating fragrance, she waited, listening. Peace because of promise was hers.

At last the sounds came; the plod of many hooves on spongy ground, an occasional lowing of cattle and the excited whinny of Pop's horse from the lot. She waited for Bronco's answering call and when his voice was heard, she rushed to stir the fire and heat the frying pan, refusing to hold back the tears of joy leaking out of her eyes and making trails on her cheeks.

She woke Ginger and sent her to help Kitty close gates and take care of Bronco.

Later Kitty would not remember staggering to the house on her sister's arm. Mom stripped off the soppy wet clothes and rubbed her down with a towel. Still shivering, but under the warmth of an old blanket, she wolfed down fried potatoes and eggs before Ginger helped her stumble across the yard to the icehouse. She stumbled down the stairs and tumbled into her bed.

Morning brought with it the patter of rain on the ice house roof. Kitty was aware of a burning stiffness in her body as she turned over, but the rhythmic tapping of the rain lulled her back to sleep.

Then she dreamed terrible visions. She was riding again and the weather had turned hot. The blazing heat burned down on her until she cried out. Then there were flames of fire, snatching at her face and she was standing at the abyss of a giant crack in the earth, watching Bronco hurtle down and down and never reaching bottom. She was weeping when the weather turned cold, freezing her until she shivered and shook. Just as suddenly she would be sweating again.

There came a time of sound sleep and then a repeat of the nightmare. Again and again it shook Kitty's body as she screamed and wept and shook.

Grace and Ginger shared turns keeping a vigil with their mother throughout the long days and nights. When their sister was hot, they wiped her face with cool water. When she was cold, they piled on blankets and coats.

"The devil is after her," Ginger exclaimed.

Grace turned wide eyes on the older sister. "What are you saying? Why would the devil be after her. She's a good girl."

"Well, something is sure chasing her."

The mother and daughters were together in the ice house in the late afternoon when Kitty's terror ended. She lay white and still, and her breathing was shallow, but she was conscious and wide awake. She was too tired to stir or even open her eyes.

"Mother, is she dead?" Grace's voice was nothing more than a whisper.

"No, only resting."

"But she looks different," Ginger could not explain why she felt so shaky.

"I know. You girls get up to the house and start some supper. I think you can throw in an extra potato. This gal will be ready to eat tonight. No, on second thought, warm up the chicken noodle soup and maybe add some water to it. We should be careful what we let her eat and the broth will be good for her."

When the girls had left the ice house the mother sat back down in the chair near the bed. "You're not in heaven." Her voice was soft and gentle as only Mom's voice could be.

"Angels could not be more beautiful," Kitty whispered, turning her head on the pillow to look at the little mother.

"You gave us quite a scare."

"I had a nightmare last night. And this is morning?"

"No, 'tis late afternoon. You've been out of your head for several days and nights, burning with fever, then shaking like a scared rabbit."

Kitty was silent for some time. When she did speak, her eyes stared off into the distance. "You're so pale, Mom. You usually don't let our being sick bother you much."

"Kitty, your Daddy died of pneumonia, complications of the flu."

"I know. Just a few months before I was born."

"Well, I also sat by his bed and helplessly watched him suffer. When he was hot, I bathed him with cool water. When he was cold, I piled on blankets and quilts. But I couldn't do a thing to help him.

Now I couldn't do anything for you either." The little mother's lips trembled.

The girl had folded her hands outside the blanket and studied them. She changed the subject, "How's Bronco?"

"Oh, he's fine. He's a tough horse and he had sense enough to wear a coat in the storm. Leave it to you to worry about a horse." Mom stood and smoothed Kitty's blankets. "Now, if you're going to be alright, I'll go up to the house and help the girls."

Kitty nodded, then called after her mother, "Hey, would you please tell Grace to make that a huge bowl of soup? I'm hungry as a bucket calf who has been locked up all night."

CHAPTER SIX

A few days later at breakfast Kitty devoured toast, scrambled eggs and coffee with a zest she had lacked before her brush with fire and rain. Her strength was returning, but still her spirit waned. She had whiled away the hours doing small chores for her mother, inspecting the new fence with Pop, who appeared delighted to show her the barbed wire and sturdy posts, and the remainder of the time she avoided quarrels with Ginger. This morning she carried a touch of excitement. Pop had asked her to ride along to Draper with him.

Ginger sulked, "I've been working hard and you haven't done a thing for a week. Seems like my turn for a rest is due."

"You have to finish cultivating the corn."

Grace was silently envious and Kitty wished the other sister could accompany them, but she knew to ask permission would be useless. She would probably have to stay home, too, if she asked for Grace's benefit.

Pop spoke little on the long road to town. The car bounced and rocked on the rutted trail and with Pop not being a pokey driver, Kitty found herself busy trying to stay on the slippery seat.

Then they roared up the main street of the dusty little town.

"Got the grocery list?" Pop asked.

Kitty nodded as the car pulled up close to the board sidewalk.

"Okay. You pick up the groceries. I'll come back and pay for them."

Kitty watched as the car jerked, backed out, then roared on down the street toward the grain elevator. She turned and entered the store.

The clerk was a young man who appeared to be a friendly chap. He seemed to be almost laughing in his glance over Kitty and of course, her blush was radiant, suddenly conscious of her bib overalls and tattered shirt.

"What can I do for you, sonny?"

Kitty bristled. "Well, sir, I need some groceries, if you can keep your snickering to a minimum long enough to pack them for me."

The clerk leaned ahead and rested his elbows on the counter, "Now I like a girl with spice. Tell me, green eyes, what are you doing this Saturday night?"

Kitty's temper flared further at the mention of the color of her eyes. "You think that is any business of yours? Here's the grocery list. Most likely, I'll be out with Bert and Dick."

The clerk's eyebrows elevated. "Two at once?"

"Sure. Takes two horses to pull a manure scraper." Kitty's mischievous side was peeping through her anger. "If you are not afraid of getting your hands dirty, you sure can join us."

"I had that coming," he grinned as he turned to the shelves and began taking down the groceries Kitty's mother had specified on the list. "I'll bet you and I could have more fun at a dance then you'll have cleaning the barn."

"You think so? Maybe I prefer the company of Bert and Dick."

"I'm wounded."

"Yah, sure, mortally, I hope," Kitty made an effort at studying the penknives in a case near her. She shrugged, "Fella, I don't even know you."

But, I know you. Brown sugar or granulated?"

"What's gram-lately?"

The clerk didn't try to hide his curiosity. "White sugar, but not powdered."

"Oh. Well, how much does the list say?"

"Ten pounds."

Kitty mentally weighed the amount, "So don't you figure Mom would want gram-lately sugar? We would never use ten pounds of powdered sugar."

"Gran-u-lated," the clerk corrected with emphasis.

"What's the difference how I say the word? I don't do the cooking. And even if I did, would there be a difference of what I called sugar?"

"I don't cook either, but I do know there is a difference in what sweetening you use for different foods. Anyway, I'd guess you best be learning to cook."

"Why?" Kitty dared him.

"Because," the clerk leaned across the counter again. "Some man is going to carry you off one of these days and you'll either cook or starve."

The haunting blush came again in spite of Kitty's wishing her face would stay pale and freckled only. "Who's dumb enough to do such a thing? You?"

"Nope." The clerk was packing the groceries in a box. "I have a girl already."

"Can she cook?"

"Come to think of it, I never asked her." The clerk was digging into his pants pocket. "You know her better than I do." He extracted a nickel from his pocket, dropped the coin into a cigar box, then picked out a candy bar from the shelf. "Give this to your sister for me, will you?"

"Which one? I have three."

"I know. One of them is in Montana. Another one I've never seen. This is for the cute little gal who wears the lavender scarf."

"Lavender scarf," Kitty echoed. "That's my lavender…" she bit off the words, picked up the candy bar and put it in a pocket on the bib of her overalls. "I'll give the candy to my mother. She's the cutest girl at our house."

"Katie? My mother has told me about her. She says your mom is one of the prettiest women in the country and works like a horse."

"Your mother is so right. And she is a good cook."

Kitty wandered over to the fabric shelf and stood looking at the bolts of cloth, daring to reach out and touch a material that grabbed her attention.

"New dress?"

"What would I do with a dress?"

The clerk drew out a bolt of crisp white and green print. He unrolled a yard or two and held the fabric near the girl's face. "This would look striking on you."

Kitty jerked back and then glanced over her shoulder to be sure Pop had not returned. "Put the cloth away."

"Sure." The clerk replaced the bolt and shrugged. He glanced beyond Kitty and whispered, "I believe I'll go dancing instead of helping you and Ginger-Pie clean the barn."

"Smart thinking. Pop wouldn't let you close to the farm, let alone in the barn with Ginger or any of the rest of us."

The clerk shrugged, "Can't win them all."

"Not a good idea to even try. But I won't tell her you are stepping out on her."

She waited for Pop to pull up to the boardwalk, and then picked up the box of groceries and went out to the car.

The evening dishes were washed before Kitty remembered the candy bar. She then waited until Pop was comfortable in his chair in the living room, cigarette smoke circling upward. Ginger and her mother were cleaning rhubarb while Grace dried and put away the dishes.

"The clerk in the store sure is a flirt," Kitty stated, then ignored Ginger's glare. She reached into her pocket and drew out the candy bar. "He told me this was for some pretty girl I know."

Grace's eyes sparkled. "Oh! Then I should have the candy."

Ginger planted herself before her youngest sister, holding out her left hand while the right hand gripped the rhubarb trimming knife. Her eyes glittered with angry unspoken thoughts, which Kitty was quite sure she did not want to hear.

She ignored her. "But he didn't say any name, so I guess he must have meant Mom." And the girl reached over to drop the bar into her mother's apron pocket before she and Grace went laughing out the door and through the darkness to their bed.

"So, you have a boyfriend?" The mother teased after the younger girls had left the kitchen.

"Oh, he's just nice to me, that's all," Ginger pouted.

"You better be getting to bed. Dawn comes early." The little mother handed Ginger the candy bar.

"Eat up, Mom. I'll share."

"No dear. I'm sure the treat was meant for you. Good night, now."

Ginger was almost out of the kitchen when her mother called softly, "Sweet dreams. Don't get chocolate on your pillow case."

In the ice house bedroom Kitty complained to Grace. "How come she gets two boyfriends and you and I have none. Tisn't fair."

"Life isn't fair," Grace answered, turned over and went to sleep.

The refreshing rain had spilled green over the land almost overnight. The grass came back, the corn tasseled and grew, wheat rippled and Mom's garden yielded bushels of vegetables.

When chilly nights indicated fall was near, the cattle were pastured at home and Kitty helped with the harvest. The girls picked cucumbers and dill for Mom's pickles. They helped can sweet corn, string beans and beets. Soon the rows of colorful jars filled the cellar shelves. Pop bought gallons of vinegar for pickling when he went to town to buy parts for the harvest machinery. Jars of tomatoes and strawberries joined the others on the shelf. Mom would sometimes stand back to survey the bounty and sigh in satisfaction.

One day Pop hollered the girls out of bed even earlier than usual. "Rustle out. Big day today."

Grace groaned and buried her face in the pillow for a moment, then climbed out and followed Kitty as they hurried to the house. "Are we cleaning the barn or did he find more fence for us to build?"

Mom was standing by the stove, frying breakfast and singing. "Dear, dear, what can the matter be? Johnny's so long at the fair."

Pop stepped up beside her, encircled her with his arm and stated in his Big Billy Goat's gruff voice. "Quit worrying about Johnny. I'm the one who's taking you to the fair."

The girls exchanged wondering looks and rushed to finish breakfast and do the chores. Kitty fed and watered the chickens while the other girls chased in the milk cows, then she hurried to the barn to help with the milking.

"Pop's mellowing," Grace whispered.

"I think the crops are causing this," Ginger replied. "He's so happy over the abundant crops, he has decided to celebrate."

"We've had good crops before," Kitty said.

Then Ginger worried. "Maybe he's afraid we'll all leave like Twyla did if he doesn't give us an occasional holiday."

"Sis didn't leave. She was sent."

"Well, she's never coming home to stay. The minute she manages to earn enough money to get back to this country she'll go get shackled to Frank."

"How do you know?"

"I feel thataway in my old bones," Ginger replied, grinning like she'd just discovered the candy dish.

They were all catching the harvest spirit. Bouncing along to town in Pop's roaring car, they tried their best to keep the dust out of their hair and off their dresses.

Kitty felt restricted and uncomfortable stuffed into a dress and wondered how her mother could bear wearing a corset. She figured Mom took off the corset before she went to bed, but otherwise she wore it everywhere, even while helping with chores.

While still a mile from town, they saw crowds of people, cars and buggies as well as horses. Excitement welled in each individual girl.

They ate their picnic lunch on the outskirts of town, spreading a tarp on the grass and feasting on Mom's fried chicken, potato salad and homemade bread. Then they packed up the empty pans and dishes and drove on to the fairgrounds.

The girls toured the women's building with their mother, admiring the needlework and rows of baked goods and canned produce.

"You should have entered some things, Mom."

"Oh, I couldn't win anything."

"You used to, long ago. But I'm guessing you didn't even know about coming to the fair in time to prepare something special."

"What do you mean, Ginger? We've been preparing stuff this good for weeks. Have you noticed the cellar shelves."

"Never mind, girls. We live so far away I wouldn't be able to get the things in before the fair and pick them up afterward."

They moved on to the buildings where livestock were housed. Kitty stood staring at a huge draft horse tied up beside a tiny pony someone had paired up for the show. "Well now," she said to Grace, "I do believe these are the big and the small of them all."

When a cry came through the crowds announcing the races were beginning, Pop came for his wife and they left the fairgrounds to go visit her relatives in town. The girls considered the duty of visiting their grandmother against seeing the horse races and the horses won. They hurried toward the grandstand, each fingering a shiny quarter Pop had handed them before he left, saying they might desire a bit of something to eat or drink before the parents returned for them.

After the children's foot races, Kitty glanced around at the crowd. Near the arched gateway of the grandstand she met the warm, brown eyes of Brice. With a casual wave he beckoned her to come to him. Kitty's heart thudded.

She jumped up, "I, I'm going back to look at the great big horse."

"By yourself?" Grace questioned.

"I'll be okay. I need you to see who wins the next race so you can tell me," she stammered before any objection could be made and then lost herself in the crowd of spectators standing about the gates.

Brice caught her hand in his when she arrived and hurried her off through the people towards the rows of parked cars. "I have something to show you."

She lengthened her stride to keep up with his and asked no questions.

She noted a man and woman standing near a car, hugging in public. When she drew back, Brice laughed and tugged her forward. His motion drew the attention of the couple, who turned to look at them. Kitty broke into a run.

She hugged Twyla to herself as her breath came in a sob. "How did you get here? When did you get here? What are you going to do?"

Twyla pushed her gently away so she could look her up and down. "Slow down, kid. Whatever happened to you over the long summer?"

"Oh, gobs of things."

"Before you get started sharing your summer," Frank interrupted with consideration for the ladies. "Suppose we get into the car where we can sit down."

Brice opened the car door and motioned Kitty into the front seat beside Twyla. "I've got to go get the team ready for the wagon race," he said, offered her a quick smile, then disappeared among the rows of cars.

"Okay," Twyla began. "I'm here because Frank ransomed me, you might say. I got here on the train last night. And what am I going to do?" Her eyes were shining as she turned to Frank. "What do you suppose I'm going to do?"

Kitty stared hard out of the window for a moment to let her feelings settle. "You will do what any girl would do if she had her hands on a guy like Frank."

"I knew you'd approve, but what about the rest of the family?"

"Grace will say, 'how wonderful' and you know what Mom will say, but…"

"He hasn't changed?"

"Not so you would notice, maybe not at all."

"I'm sorry, sorry for you girls."

Kitty shook her head, "Don't be. When the time is right, there is nothing to stop at least one of those girls from leaving, and I think the others probably feel the same way I do."

She lingered to brief her oldest sister on the events of the summer, and then she hurried back to the grandstand to watch the horse races.

When she ducked through the gate of the grandstand she saw her place beside Ginger had been taken by a young man, the storekeeper from town. Grace caught her eye and grinned, so Kitty nodded and found a place near the bottom of the tiered seats.

She hollered with the rest of the crowd during the races, picking out her favorites and cheering them on. When the time came for the wagon pulling race, she screamed loudest for the gleaming chestnut geldings and they won. After the finish, without thinking, she ducked out through the crowds again and made her way to the west end of the grandstand. Catching up a gunny sack, she helped Brice rub down the chestnut horses.

"Tomboy," he teased, "you'll get your dress dirty."

Kitty hesitated, and looked down at the dress her cousin had given her, a dress which had become too tight on a girl who had fit into it with room to spare just a year ago. She shrugged, "I'm more comfortable doing this then I would be if I were standing around waving a little fan and gossiping."

"Can't quite picture you in that frame," he smiled.

"The only thing better than this would be to be the one behind a winning team. But then, I would not want to go up against you."

"Do you drive teams at home?"

"Not really. I do the pitching hay on and pitching hay off, like when we are feeding cows in the wintertime. And since I've spent my latest summers riding herd on the cows, I haven't been involved much with haying. Ginger usually gets to do the driving while Grace and I get the grunt work."

"Well, I will have to see that you get some driving time."

She didn't ask for details. When they finished rubbing down the horses, he left her beside the handsome team and went off through the people. A little later he returned, bearing large glasses of cool lemonade. Kitty savored each sip as they leaned against the hay rack the team had pulled in their winning race. His brown, laughing eyes studied her until she blushed and picked at the bits of horse hair clinging to her skirt. "I don't think I've ever seen such a beautiful team of horses."

Brice nodded. "Sadly, I'm soon to lose them."

"Why?" Kitty was alarmed.

"Williams has sold them to some rich guy from the East."

"Oh," she cried, "how can he bear to let them go?"

"Eight hundred dollars will buy a lot of horse feed with plenty left over for people feed."

"Eight hundred..." Kitty's breath rushed out in a low whistle.

Brice shrugged, "If they were mine, I wouldn't part with them for even a lot more than that. I don't believe they could lay down enough money for this team if they were mine."

Kitty considered his statement. "No, I guess not. Some things just can't be bought."

"I guess the fact they belong to someone else is just as well. They are well trained and I've already started a team of bay colts, and there is a black team coming up for next spring."

"You like working with horses, don't you?"

"Yes. So do you."

She nodded. Then she helped him lead the team to one of the horse barns where they were taken into a large stall and tied loosely to a manger where they could munch on fresh hay.

"I have a feeling I ought to be looking for my sisters," Kitty worried. "I expect the folks will be ready to go soon."

"You're not staying for the harvest festival?"

"What's the harvest festival?"

"A party, you might say. Let me show you where the dancing is held." He led her to a bowery and showed her the platform, built well from solid wood and raised a few inches off the ground. "Come dark, the people gather here and dance under the stars."

"Sounds like fun, but I've never danced."

"Don't believe in it?"

She laughed, "I didn't know dancing was supposed to be sinful until I read that in a book. I've just recently learned a new love for God, you see, and I found some interesting items in a book Frank sent over, but parts of the book and I don't agree."

He nodded, "I play with a dance band quite often, and I see things I don't approve of once in a while, but dance in itself isn't so bad; most dancing anyway. But aside from dancing, what do you mean you have a new love for God?"

Confronted with his direct questioning, Kitty was at a loss for words. She sat down on the step of the bowery and clasped her hands in front of her. He leaned against a post nearby, picked up a wood shaving and began to peel off strips with his pocket knife.

She struggled to find the right words. "Once I read the story of Nicodemus in Mom's Bible. Mom and my real daddy got a Bible from my daddy's mom and dad for a wedding present," she wasn't sure why she felt she had to explain that. "Anyway, seems how this man came to Jesus and asked him how to get to heaven and Jesus said you have to be born again. And I wondered how I could be born again." Kitty's words rushed on. "Finally, I realized this new life comes from just giving yourself to Jesus and asking Him to be your Savior. Do you get what I'm trying to say?"

"Yes," he held up the wood and studied his carving. "I understand, and I'm glad." Suddenly startled, he dropped the shaving on her lap and hurried away from the bowery.

Kitty looked up to see her family approaching from the grandstand. She peeked behind her to be sure Brice was out of sight. As the group approached, they were laughing and talking with abandon as they came toward her and Pop teased, "I should have known better than to bring my little hayseed to town. She couldn't stand the crowds and had to get away by herself."

"By herself, tee hee," Grace giggled in Kitty's ear on the way to the car.

She ignored her sister as she clutched the smooth little piece of wood Brice had carved. She reviewed the day and sighed, only because the end had come all too soon.

CHAPTER SEVEN

Winter swept down on them in early November with a day-long blizzard and howling winds blasting high drifts out from the southeast corner of buildings.

The next morning, Kitty chose the lowest parts of the drifts and waded through them to care for the chickens before breakfast. The hens gathered around and pecked snow off her boots as she measured grain into their feeder. The rooster crowed his welcome to the snowy day and his lady friends seemed to agree the day wasn't so bad after all.

Kitty moved on to the barn to help her sisters with their chores. When the milking was done, the girls trudged back to the house where Mom had cooked farina and fried slabs of home-cured ham to accompany scrambled eggs. The aroma of fresh brewed coffee hurried them to the breakfast table.

The remainder of the morning was spent by Kitty and Grace helping Pop feed the cattle while Ginger stayed in the house and practiced the finer arts of baking. Pop grumbled about the early storm, worrying aloud if the hay would ever last until green grass came when one had to start feeding the cattle in November. They pitched hay off the stacks into the rack to which the team had been hitched. When the rack was full, Pop drove the team out into the home pasture and the girls pitched the hay down to the snowy ground. The cattle followed the horses and rack, pushing each other and rushing to get the choicest bits of hay.

When the team was unharnessed, the girls rubbed down the horses, tied them to the manger and then pitched hay down for them from the loft.

On the way to the house Grace caught up a handful of snow and threw the white fluff into Kitty's face. The younger girl stopped, sputtered, and then ran to catch Grace before she reached the porch. They tumbled and rolled in the snow, laughing, squealing and poking the powdery cold stuff into any place they could find. Grace screamed when Kitty shoved snow into the neck of her jacket.

When they stomped their feet on the porch, Mom came out with the broom and swept the snow from their coats and coveralls, scolding in fun and giving a quick spank of the broom to their backsides.

They sat down to a hearty dinner of ham and beans, hot bread rolls direct from the oven, and tall glasses of milk. Dessert was a carrot cake made by Ginger and even Kitty had to praise the cake's fine moist texture.

When the dishes were cleared away and washed, Grace brought out a much-used jigsaw puzzle, which she, Teddy and Kitty worked at putting together while Ginger sat nearby embroidering a dishtowel. Pop had built a roaring fire in his shop stove and was out there mending harness.

Suddenly Grace slammed her hand down flat on the table, scattering puzzle pieces. "I miss Twyla."

Mom looked up in surprise, and then turned back to her sock mending without answer. Kitty stared with open mouth at Grace.

When the startle wore off Ginger, she mocked. "Oh, she's probably married off to some handsome young man and they're settled in their snug little cabin in the Montana mountains."

Kitty had become very busy looking for a certain puzzle piece. Her secret welled up and pushed to be let out, but she kept her eyes downcast and her mouth shut.

"Her marrying Frank would sure defeat Pop's purpose in sending her away," said Grace. "Mom, can't you get her back?"

"I suppose I could, if I asked Pop. But do you think that is the best option for her?"

"No," Grace answered after a moment of consideration. "I guess not. But this is sure going to be a long winter without her."

The second snowstorm of the season was raging when they awoke on Thanksgiving morning.

"Looks like we are in for a long, hard winter," Pop grumbled, shivering as he stoked a roaring fire in the cook stove.

At noon there was roast chicken with dressing, mashed potatoes and gravy to highlight the Thanksgiving dinner. Kitty carried up pickles and beans from the cellar. And the family sampled the youngest girl's first attempt at pumpkin pie.

The making of the crust had nearly ended any enthusiasm she had for baking. She had carefully measured flour and salt into Mom's green bowl, then added home-rendered lard. With knife and fork she cut the fat into the flour, but the mixture looked really greasy. Then she added a couple spoons full of water, which she had added to a well-beaten egg and a splash of vinegar.

While she had struggled to turn the mix into a ball, Mom added a bit more water, which worked, of course. She had floured the table and dumped the dough out, only to be convinced there must be a naughty elf sitting on Mom's rolling pin.

"Dweebs, I can handle a pitchfork better than I can a rolling pin. My husband is not going to get pie…ever."

Ginger snorted. "You better worry about getting a husband before you worry about making him a pie."

"Ah, nothing to it." She had flopped the pieces of crust into the pie plate and worked it with her fingers until there was no tin showing. "I absolutely refuse to be an old maid. I will find someone who doesn't care if I can bake a pie." She artfully worked the crust edge in a fancy spiral around the pan.

After carefully pouring in the pumpkin filling Grace had assembled for her, she put the pie in the oven where it baked to perfection.

Pop's compliment to her was to take a second piece, topped with whipped cream.

And Teddy said, "When I grow up and get my ranch, you can come to Texas and be my cook."

"You don't need Texas," Pop informed his son. "You know this place is going to be yours in a few years."

The boy had sense enough not to answer.

♪ ♪ ♪

The storm was still blowing fiercely when the girls went out to do evening chores. The wind sucked away Kitty's breath and threatened to throw her to the ground. She clung to milk buckets in one hand and with the other held tight to Ginger as the three girls pressed together through the swirling, blinding storm. They couldn't see the barn until the building loomed right in front of them.

The howling wind demanded the strength of all three young women to get the barn door open wide enough to squeeze through before it banged shut again.

"Wow," Ginger panted when they slipped inside the barn, "We'd better be careful going back to the house. Another three feet and we would have missed the barn. We should have tied a rope to the porch pillar for something to hang on to."

They pitched down hay into the mangers and measured oats into the milk cows' feed boxes. Kitty had brought a carrot from the house. She snapped the treat in pieces and fed it to Bert and Dick. The team took the pieces from her palm and munched them.

Since only two cows were producing at the moment, milking did not take long. The other four milk cows were awaiting new calves within the month.

The girls dreaded the struggle to get back to the house.

Ginger stood still, thinking. Finally, she suggested, "Why can't we take some of the rope we use to roll the hay up into the loft?"

"Do you think we can tie that big stuff"

"I think so. We don't dare try cutting it. Pop would have our hide."

"You really think we can carry that heavy old rope and still find the door of the house?"

"What can we tie it to?"

"Take this end of the rope." Ginger ordered Grace. "Go out the door and try to go straight ahead to reach the hitching rail in front of the barn. If you find it, wrap the rope around the rail and tie a square knot. You know how to tie a square knot, right?"

"Do I look dumb?"

"No comment." Ginger turned to Kitty. "Take the other end and get the next rope. Tie the two together with a square knot."

"Yes, I know how to tie a square knot. Do you think you are the only one who knows anything around this place?"

"I was the one who figured out a way to get back to the house without getting lost."

"Providing we can find the house."

"We will find the house. We will keep following the rope back to the hitching rail and trying again until we get to the house."

"What if the rope won't reach from the barn to the house?"

"There is an older rope hanging on the gate in the middle part of the barn. Go get it. We will tie it on right now."

By the time Kitty came back to the door with a third rope, Grace swept in with the wind. "I got it tied to the hitching post."

"Did you tie it in a square knot?" Kitty dramatized in falsetto voice.

"Oh, shut up. As soon as we get this other rope tied on, I'll wrap it around myself and break a trail. After a bit, you come next, Grace. Hang on to a pail of milk with one hand and wrap the rope around your other arm. Kitty, bring the other pail of milk. Whatever you guys do, don't drop the rope. Let go of the buckets and hang on with both hands if you have to."

Ginger tied a knot in the loose end of the rope, wrapped it around her waist and tied it again. "You two help me shove all this rope outside. And then you pray if you know how. You pray I can find the house on the first try. Give me some time, then you head out."

It took two girls to hold the door open against the wind while the third drug the rope outside and piled it up. Ginger disappeared into the swirling white blindness.

It seemed forever before Grace felt a pull on the other end of the rope. "Let's go. She made it."

"Thank you, God." Kitty hollered, slipped out the door behind Grace and securely shut it before looping her left arm over the lifesaving rope.

When they at last managed to get back into the house, Ginger cried. "You spilled the milk."

"I did not!" Grace retorted, then looking down, she saw both pails were almost empty.

"Oh my," said Mom. "I should have sent covered syrup pails with you. The wind has sucked the milk right out of your buckets."

The weeks before Christmas were busy with little secrets. The girls sewed a new apron for Mom and Ginger embroidered big red poinsettias on the pocket. They made large fancy stitches on strips of narrow elastic to make sleeve garters for Pop.

"I just can't think of anything for Ginger," Grace lamented one afternoon as the two youngest girls sat on the floor of Mom's bedroom. "She can dig down in her dresser drawer and come up with something she has embroidered for us, but what can we give her?"

Kitty leaned against the bed, "If there wasn't so much snow, maybe Pop would take us to town and we could buy her something."

"With what? Our good looks? I don't have any money."

"I have my quarter from the fair."

"I saw you drinking lemonade. How did you have lemonade and keep your quarter? Did you steal when the man wasn't looking?"

"You ought to know me better. I would not steal anything. I might tell you someday how I got lemonade, but since you are already accusing me of something anyway, I'm not going to bother to tell you now."

"Oh simmer, you bad-tempered brat." Grace shrugged, "Oh well, thinking about shopping in a store is no use. We're almost out of flour and if Pop can't get to town for flour, he sure can't get there for little nothings we might want to give for Christmas gifts. Sometimes I hate snow, I hate cold and I hate winter."

Kitty poked at the rag bag while trying to think of something creative, but then grabbed the bag and dumped the contents on to the floor. She and Grace spied Mom's old silk print dress at the same instant and their eyes met.

"Silk wouldn't make a good rag, anyway," Grace said as she picked up Mom's shears.

They cut a large square from the least worn part of the skirt, then stitched a narrow hem around the edge to make a scarf for Ginger.

"Now maybe she'll quit taking my lavender one."

One evening Mom called Kitty into her bedroom where she handed the girl several sheets of pale pink stationery. "Why not make an autograph book for Grace?"

"Hey, good idea." Kitty busied herself, carefully cutting the pages in half. She fashioned covers from cloth glued to cardboard and carefully lettered "Pals and Poems" on the front along with Grace's name. “Strange,” she thought, “but since we got out of grade school there hasn’t been much opportunity for autographs. Grace will have to keep these pages blank until she breaks her ties.” She punched holes in the pages and the covers and tied them together with a length of ribbon from Mom’s sewing collection.

Then she chose a page near the middle of the booklet and wrote in her best handwriting:

“First comes love, then comes marriage, then comes Gracie with a baby carriage.” After that she wrote, “I wish you luck, I wish you joy, I wish you first a baby boy. And when his hair begins to curl, I wish you then a baby girl. And when she’s through with diaper pins, I wish you then a pair of twins.”

She signed her name and added a decorative swirl.

Christmas day dawned with brilliant sunshine. The chores were done in a hurry and dinner started.

They were preparing to sit down and eat when Kitty glanced out a window and saw horses coming across the pasture. She squealed “company” and everybody crowded around the window.

The horses were pulling a lightweight, old-fashioned cutter. The little sleigh sped over the snow and stopped before the house where the whole family was already out on the porch.

Frank leaped out, ran around the other side of the cutter and swung Twyla up on to the porch. Pop gave the girl a quick hug, then grabbed his coat and went with Frank to the barn to unhitch the horses and rub them down before finding a measure of oats for each.

The girls ushered Twyla into the house and began removing layer after layer of warm woolen coats, scarves and sweaters, until she stood, dainty and pretty in a brown dress accented by delicate lace collar and cuffs.

Ginger spun her around, “Oh, you look positively radiant. Montana must have agreed with you.”

Sunlight flashed on something on Twyla’s left hand. Grace was the first to catch hold of the hand, “I know why she’s so pretty.” Close inspection by all the girls revealed a white gold band on her third finger.

"Shucks," Grace teased. "You've been given a piece of wire. I could have made you one myself."

"Tisn't the ring that counts, girls, but the man," Mom confided. "Forty years from now, Lord willing, Twyla will still have both the ring and the man. Now let's get dinner on the table."

Twyla had brought a cake decorated with white icing and tiny red candies. She lifted the cake carefully from one of the boxes Frank brought in from the sleigh.

"Birthday cake?" quizzed Grace.

"Aren't we celebrating Jesus' birthday?" Twyla asked.

Excitement trickled around the dinner table. Twyla told about her summer in Montana where the ranches spilled out for miles. Frank had bits of news from town, including a Christmas greeting from the girls' grandmother.

When the dishes were done, the gifts were brought to the table. Mom exclaimed over her apron. Kitty had a scarf identical to the one she and Grace had made for Ginger. Each girl had an embroidered dresser scarf from Ginger. Pop handed out envelopes each having two crisp dollar bills tucked inside.

Then Mom opened a mysterious package. Inside was a wooden box with blunted nails standing on their heads under the lid. "A spool box," she exclaimed. There was also an envelope in the spool box, and inside was a catalog clipping of a pretty dress along with ten dollars. Mom leaned over and squeezed Pop's hand.

Twyla had brought Ginger and Grace agate string bracelets. There was a headscarf for Mom, which had the word "Montana" painted on each side. Pop's present was a bright tie with a painting of Old Faithful spouting off. Then Twyla presented Kitty with a picture folder.

The girl touched the cover reverently. "Grand Tetons," she breathed softly, "just as I've always imagined they looked." When she opened the booklet, Grace leaned over and pointed. "There's your cowboy! See, he's even waving at you."

Kitty blushed, and hugged Twyla.

"I'd like to look at your pitchers," Teddy exclaimed, "as soon as you get done with the book, of course."

Then nighttime came. After supper and chores the family gathered in the kitchen again. Mom brought her Bible to Frank and the young man read the Christmas story.

Then Mom turned down the kerosene lamp until there was only a faint glow in the room and they sang carols and winter lyrics, including "Jingle Bells" and "O Christmas Tree."

"Did you know," offered Frank. "Jingle Bells was actually written as a Thanksgiving Song? And O Tannenbaum was not referring to what we know as a Christmas tree. Being a fir, it was noted for its strength and endurance."

"Just as we should be known for standing strong in our faith in Jesus."

Outside the window, the moon turned the snow to glitter. Kitty's heart ached against her throat. She believed Christmas would never again be the same as it was on this peaceful night.

The girls slept on blankets on the kitchen floor to give Frank and Twyla their bedroom. Before they slept, Twyla came out to the kitchen in her long flannel nightgown. She sat on the floor with her sisters in front of the cook stove.

"Tell us about your wedding," Grace said.

"There isn't much to tell. Kitty has probably told you I got back at fair time…"

"Fair time?" echoed Ginger and Grace. They turned on Kitty. "You mean you knew all this time she was home?"

Kitty nodded.

"Quit interrupting," Twyla instructed. "Anyway, I went to work for Frank's aunt until we got the first snowstorm, then I went to Frank's home. One morning his mother said, 'This weather isn't fit for getting any work done. You two might as well go get married.' So we did."

Grace leaned back against her pillow as Ginger stated, "I told you guys she'd come back and marry Frank."

The two youngest girls exchanged private smiles, but did not comment.

Frank and Twyla left in the morning. Just before their departure, Pop turned to Frank. "I think you know I do not think this marriage was a good idea. I'm not sure you have what it takes to make a good home for this gal." Then he nodded to Twyla, "You can always come home, you know."

"Oh dweebs," Kitty muttered before slamming back into the house.

It seemed Frank and Twyla had taken the sunshine from the house. The youngest sisters moped around until Pop sent them to clean the chicken coop.

And the winter wore on.

The hours melted into days and nights, then weeks. Kitty lost herself whenever possible in the books Frank had loaned her on Christmas Day.

Her birthday came in March and there was a cake with eighteen candles. Late in the night she lay awake, fighting down an ache of loneliness, which made her want to cry. She could not have explained the feeling or the cause if anyone had asked. She did not know what she was longing for. How could one live in a house full of people and still feel lonely?

At last the final snowstorm came. And with the blizzard came the first calves from the range cows; two tiny wet bundles of red and white softness. The girls carried them into the house and rubbed them down with gunny sacks. After roping together the kitchen chairs to make a pen so the babies would not get too close to the cook stove, they were left as near to the fire as possible to dry out and warm up.

The girls took turns throughout the day and night, going out and searching through the cattle herd for more calves. The rain and snow soaked their clothes and chilled their bones, but no more calves were born during the blizzard.

At dawn the storm was rain only, melting the snow and running in rivulets off the cattle's steaming backs. The creeks rose rapidly, carrying dirty swirling water and chunks of ice.

Ginger shivered, a blue line of cold around her mouth. "This stuff will kill a calf faster than a blizzard."

Kitty nodded. "We could pray for them."

"What good would praying do?" Ginger sniffed.

"Let's cut out the heaviest cows and put them in the north end of the barn. You guard the gate and I'll pick out the ones who are going to calve first."

"Good luck," Kitty scorned. "You know the ones you lock up almost never are the next to calf."

They sloshed through the mud and goo and were soaked again before the job was finished.

Several hours later another calf was born, out in the lot. Ginger and Kitty stood in the rain and shook their heads. "You could lock up every cow but one in the barn and who would have a calf?" Kitty asked.

"The one outside, naturally."

"I told you so," she muttered, but Ginger had already walked away. "And I'm still going to keep praying for them."

When Kitty went out at midnight the rain had stopped and the moon was so bright she did not need to light the lantern until she stepped into the barn. She could hear the rush of the creek in the distance. The fresh damp odor of a wet world filled her nostrils and gave her a heady feeling.

In the barn a cow was busy licking a newborn calf. Kitty grabbed a relatively clean gunny sack, wrapped it around the wet baby, picked him up and carried him into a smaller pen where he would not be trampled by the herd. His mother followed, sounding maternal protests.

At last the days grew warmer and green grass sprouted up everywhere. Mom made out an order for garden seeds. Pop and Ginger went to town and came home with more fencing supplies. Kitty's heart ached. The fence meant an end of her herding days. She maintained a halfhearted effort as she helped build the fence; setting and tamping posts, stringing wire, stretching wire, building gates.

"Why do they call that a dead man?" Teddy inquired as he helped Kitty wrap wire around a heavy piece of old iron, drop it in to a hole and tamp in dirt, leaving the wire sticking out. That end of the wire was wrapped snugly around the gate post and then stapled into place.

"Dunno. Why don't you ask your daddy?" She put a short stick between the folds of wire and wound it round and round, tightening the fence. "Or better yet, use your imagination to figure out the answer."

When her spirits lagged Mom threatened to feed her a spring tonic.

"Made of mustard greens and rusty nails," Grace teased.

The days of spring turned to summer and Kitty worked hard to do her part at building the fence, but her enthusiasm for the job was nonexistent.

One afternoon she walked toward the house through the warm sunshine, carrying a jar to refill with drinking water at the pump. So it happened she overheard snatches of conversation when she passed the shop.

"I don't know what's wrong with her," Pop grumbled. "She ought to be getting over spring fever by now."

"Maybe if you'd send her out with the cattle."

"Which couldn't last more than a month or so. Herding cattle in this country ends with the building of fences."

"Well, I don't know," Mom sighed, "but we're losing her. She'll be gone at the first opportunity. There's something out there she wants."

Kitty could not hear Pop's grumbling reply. She hurried away, hoping the couple would not realize she had heard them discussing her state of mind. Her face was flushed and hot, but not from sunshine.

On a morning several days later Kitty went to the barn shortly after noon. She had been left without any orders, so after she washed dishes and straightened the kitchen, she went out to brush the saddle horses. Pop and Ginger had gone to work on the fence while Mom and Grace were in the garden.

She found the horses in the barn, stomping their feet and switching tails at flies. She slipped a halter on Bronco and tied him securely to a feed rack, then chased the other horses into another part of the barn and fastened the gate of separation.

When she slid back the big barn door, the sunshine and fresh air streamed in and Kitty sang as she curried Bronco's hair.

After a bit she laid down the curry comb and using her pocket knife as a tool, she pulled the cockle burrs from Bronco's mane and tail.

Bronco's sudden whinny startled Kitty and she looked up to see the horse had turned his head to look out the doorway. Then the thud of horses' hooves came to her ears.

Puzzled, she walked over to look outside.

The horses appeared to be the bay team from the Williams Ranch. She knew Pop had talked of buying them. On his most recent trip to town he must have stopped in at the ranch and made arrangements for the purchase. Now a certain young man was riding one of the big horses and leading the other.

Kitty ran out to open the gate and felt her heart take a strange dive as she looked up into Brice's brown eyes.

"Hi Kitty," his smile sparked warmth all through her. "I brought you a present."

"A present, huh? Well, I guess that must be so because Pop sure didn't say anything to me about buying horses."

Brice slid off his big mount, "I wish they were mine to give away. Because if they were, I sure wouldn't."

"Not even to me?" she teased.

"Well, maybe," he answered, turning to shut the gate, "but only on certain conditions."

"Such as?"

"Time will tell." He changed the subject. "Should I turn the team loose in here?"

"Might as well." Kitty wiped the blade of her jackknife on a pant leg, closed the knife and dropped the tool into her pocket.

"I thought Ole would be here with the pickup before I arrived. I guess I made better time than he thought I would." Brice ambled over to the doorway of the barn. "You the only one around here?"

Kitty dared, "Do you think I could be standing here talking to you if I weren't?"

Brice pushed back his straw hat to study Kitty. "Sister or Pop?"

Kitty shrugged before walking past the young man into the barn. "Both. One or the other, doesn't make much difference." Then picking up the curry comb, she proceeded to brush Bronco's back legs and comb his tail.

"You could get kicked," Brice suggested.

"I could—accidentally. Bronco might be ornery sometimes, but kicking ain't one of his games."

"He's the one who whinnied for you after the two of you rolled down the creek bank?"

Kitty paused to look at the man. "How did you know 'bout that?"

"Heard Twyla telling Frank."

"You see quite a bit of them?"

"Who?" he quizzed.

"Frank and Twyla."

"Sometimes."

Kitty had returned to grooming the horse when his question again stopped her. "Were you surprised when they got married?"

She was glad her face was hidden by Bronco's flank. "Sorta, sorta not. Montana is a long way away."

"Love is strong."

"Did you read that in some book?" She met his eyes for a passing moment.

"Read what?"

"About love?" Kitty untied Bronco's lead rope. Brice did not answer as she led the horse into the yard and freed him to make an acquaintance with the team.

"I reckon I probably did read the words. But you can also see such love between people if you know what you are looking for."

"Then you yourself have never been in love?" Kitty could scarcely believe her own voice had posted the question. A sort of magnetism drew her to glance at the young man and his eyes seemed to pierce her in return.

"Been in love? No. Am in love? Maybe."

A shiver crept down over Kitty and she looked away.

He changed the subject. "So, tell me about your horses?"

"I don't have a horse."

He smiled, sort of. "The ones you work with."

"Okay. Well, you've already met Broncho. He was my daddy's colt, but he died before he had a chance to do any training other than halter break."

"So, he is about eighteen, then?"

"Close enough. The horse in back of the barn is Pop's. He's ornery as all get out. I don't ride him if I can help it. But he does seem to appreciate my curry comb." She nodded toward the east. "That mangy creature in the corner is Teddy's dashing steed."

"I take it you don't have a particular love for Shetlands."

"Not that one, anyway. I've never been around any others." She glanced about them before lowering her voice. "Gotta tell you what I saw shortly after that critter came here. But you can't tell anyone I told you, not even Frank."

He slashed his finger in an "X" across his chest. "But if Twyla knows, you can bet Frank does."

"I imagine. Anyway, Teddy rides the pony to school, you see. Well, the first day he headed down the hill at a trot and Teddy was hanging on for dear life, trying to stay on the horse, slow him down and keep track of his lunch bucket all at once. So the pony slams on the brakes at the bridge. No way is that dinky piece of horseflesh going to go across that bridge. Teddy is kicking him and yelling and he just bunches up his little belly and doesn't budge."

Kitty lowered her voice even more. "Teddy didn't see Pop a'coming down the hill, but the pony did. Just as Pop lets fly with a kick at the pony's rump, the pony jumps to the side. Teddy falls off and Pop falls down. I plugged my ears until the smoke cleared."

He was laughing. She added, "Life actually can get pretty loopy around here."

Before he could respond, she blurted. "Here comes your boss's noisy car."

"Kitty, I…"

"Here comes Pop, too, and Ginger. End of conversation." She fled into the shaded depths of the barn.

With trembling hands she began to clean cockle burrs from the tail of Pop's horse, being careful of his back feet only because of long habit. What meaning was behind that glimpse she had seen? Who could he love? She remembered the afternoon of fishing the summer before and the picnic Ginger had gone to. Could he really love her sister? Could he?

Of course he could. If the horse had been her gentle Bronco, Kitty might have hidden her face against him and let the tears rain.

After a while Ginger appeared at the barn door and hollered back into the dimness of afternoon shade. "Hey stuck up. Do you know we have company? Come be sociable."

"No."

Ginger shrugged and turned back to join the three men. Pop issued an order to her. "Let the team and Bronco out through the north gate, then watch to see if the gelding leads the team to the dam to drink."

"Okay."

Kitty watched over the horse's back until Brice left with Ginger and the animals, then she emerged from the barn and squatted in the shade while pulling horse hair from the curry comb. Mr. Williams smiled a warm greeting in her direction. She nodded and smiled in return.

She was leaning back against the barn soaking up the warmth of the sunshine when the returning sound of voices stirred her thoughts. She resisted the impulse to flee back into the shady coolness of the barn and hide.

Mom's laughter and Grace's chatter proved the gardeners had joined Brice and Ginger somewhere along the way. They paused on the other side of the gate, but Kitty did not look up until an awareness of someone's eyes on her caused the color to feed into her face. Without moving her head, she lifted her eyes to once again meet the warm darkness of those of the young man. She noticed too, the slight smile, which gave her the impression of a cat mauling a mouse. Pop's speaking to his visitor halted the girl's quick rise of fury.

"Let's go to the house and I'll write you a check," the little fellow ordered. "Ginger, rustle over there and mix up some lemonade."

Brice fell in beside the three other adults as they walked toward the house. Kitty's eyes noted Pop slipping his arm around her mother, a gesture so seldom displayed the girl wondered if the buying of the new team was something to celebrate or if Pop was trying to impress someone. Since she had never known him to celebrate having to spend money, she figured the gesture was intended for show.

"Well, I'll celebrate all right," she muttered, jumping to her feet and slinging the curry comb at the fence. The tool crashed and fell in two pieces for which in an instant Kitty was ashamed of her temper. Glad no one had looked back, she hurried over to pick up the pieces. She figured she was lucky the handle had only slipped out of its groove and was easy for her to replace. She jammed the curry comb back into the handle with a rap on the board fence and returned to the barn to release Pop's horse.

"As I was saying," she continued, and had an impulse to laugh, "I might be privileged enough to celebrate by driving the new team to pull the manure spreader. What a waste. These beauties ought to be pulling a carriage made for two or something more exciting than doing farm work."

Kitty turned Pop's horse loose and stood for a long time, staring out over the prairie and wondering about the feeling tumbling through her insides. She did not believe she was longing to mount Bronco and herd cattle again. And just as well for her sake, for those days were gone and would not return. Fences had canceled the purpose of herding cattle on open prairie.

The girl dawdled until curiosity seized her and she started toward the house, hands deep in her pockets, head bent forward until the damp, brown curls of her forehead fell free. She encountered Mr. Severson by the path leading up to the porch, waiting for Brice to bring the pickup from near the barn.

"Miss Kitty, the winter wheat is nearly ripe, nearly ready to be harvested. When the threshers come my wife could use a helper. Would you be interested in coming to work on the Williams Ranch?"

Kitty's heart struck up a thumping tune. "Did you ask Pop?"

"No," he smiled. "It's you I want to hire, not Pop."

Then he continued. You seem to think for yourself. I thought at your age your future would be your business."

"I d-don't know if I can leave here," she stammered.

"Well, you see what you can do. Finding help at this time of year isn't easy, so I'm sure the job will be waiting for you and available until after corn is picked this fall."

He continued, “Feeding the harvest crew makes quite a load on my wife.”

“I’ll see what happens,” Kitty added while unable to lift her eyes to his face. “Maybe if I can’t come, I can think of someone who can.”

“If your leaving would mean you cannot return here when the harvest is finished,” he ventured, “we can get you a job over at the Murdo House. I have friends there, you know.”

“No, I didn’t know.”

“Come if you can.”

“I don't know much about cooking.”

“My wife would be pleased to teach you, and she is one of the best. And now, good day.” His voice rose above the roar of the approaching auto. “I sure hope the team pleases you.” Then he got into the pickup and the outfit rattled off down the road.

“Well, he might have waved goodbye,” Ginger said as she came to stand beside Kitty.

“Who?”

“Well, who do you suppose?” snorted the sister.

“Sure doesn't make any difference to me if Mr. Severson waved or not.”

“Very funny. You know who I was talking about. By the way,” Ginger snapped, “what were you and he talking about?”

“Who?”

“Who, who, who? Do your feet fit a limb?”

Kitty was busy shifting her bare feet in the dusty road, using one to heap dirt on the other. She did not answer as soon as Ginger thought she should, and before she did, Pop and Grace had come from the house.

“Well?” Ginger prodded.

“We were discussing…” Kitty took her time composing an answer, “at the rate water flows over the VanHueven Dam, how long would it take to fill a shotgun bucket with rose petals.” Kitty shook the dust from each foot and strolled away from her sister, who for once was speechless.

After supper Kitty approached Pop. The dishes had been washed and when she had swept the floor and put away the broom, she went out on to the porch where he sat in the darkness, appreciating an occasional cool breath of air. The house grew as quiet as the last part of death. Knowing the rest of the family was going to hear every word she and Pop exchanged, she drew a deep breath and almost changed her mind.

She stepped into the shadows away from the door where he could not see her pale face. “Mr. Severson asked me to come help his missus during harvest.”

“I need you here.”

“Then you're saying you don’t want me to go?”

“I’m surprised you even asked.”

“So am I.” Kitty jumped off the side of the porch and disappeared into the darkness.

CHAPTER EIGHT

Sometime later when Grace lit the lantern in the ice house bedroom she found her little sister lying on the bed fully clothed, staring at the roof overhead.

“You ought to get mad more often,” Grace commented as she took her time getting ready for bed.

“Why?”

“You’re quite pretty with your face all pale and those marble eyes snapping fire.”

Kitty grinned.

“And what’s so funny about what I just said?”

“Your nice way of talking about my eyes. Your comment didn’t register with me right away, but I too have played marbles enough to know all about cat’s eyes. Cousin Dell could take a lesson in niceness from you. She used to call me Cat Eyes when we were in school together.” Kitty undressed, put out the lamp and got into bed beside Grace.

Soon Grace’s voice came in the darkness. “Kitty, where is the VanHueven Dam?”

“I don’t know,” Kitty laughed. “I think I read where a fellow told his girl he’d love her until the VanHueven Dam went dry: 'tis probably a little dirt grade across a creek in someone’s pasture.”

"I bet they throw nosy people in there."

After a long silence, Grace spoke again. "Sister, a bird never knows how far she can fly until she tries her wings."

"So why don't you take your own advice?"

"I haven't been offered an opportunity like you heard today. Besides, I don't have the nerve…yet. I will, though. I just need a little more time."

"You think I have the nerve to leave without his permission?"

"Yes."

Long, work-filled days passed. It seemed Pop found the dirtiest jobs he could for the youngest of the sisters.

Then one morning Kitty showed up late for breakfast. She washed her hands and face at the bench, then sat down at the table, but did not take any food.

"I'm…" her voice failed. Grace bent her head over her plate. Ginger's eyes on Kitty held a suspicious gleam.

"I'm going to work on the Williams Ranch."

"You wouldn't dare," Ginger blurted. "Why, you…" She was silenced by Pop's glare.

The man's voice came across as steady, controlled, but Kitty saw the purple tinge of wrath on his face. "So you've decided to leave home. Well, I think you've spent too much time loafing lately. There is a field of corn you can weed. You'll find the hoe in the shop."

"Weed the corn by hand," Grace echoed, unbelieving, and then wished she could crawl under the table to avoid the glares she received.

"I've made up my mind," Kitty stated without hesitation, her face growing redder by shades. She stood up, but not trusting her trembling legs to support her, she leaned against the table. "Will you drive me over there?"

"I should say not," Pop roared, leaping to his feet and spilling his chair behind him. He shook his fist in Kitty's face. "Get out, little girl, and don't you come back. I don't care if you end up hungry and penniless, don't come begging to me. I've given you all you'll ever get from me." The door slammed behind him as he stomped from the house.

"I'm sorry, Mom." Kitty cried, then she also ran from the kitchen.

Her packing took little time or effort. She included her two cotton dresses, her only pair of shoes and four stockings, but decided there was no sense taking the party dress cousin Dell gave her. The garment was too tight, too short, and she would have no place to wear a fancy dress if it did fit. She stuffed her meager belongings into a flour sack pillowcase as Ginger entered the ice house bedroom and plunked herself on the bed.

"What a way to show your gratitude for all Pop has done for us."

"He doesn't need me. You can just work a little harder."

"As if I didn't already do more than my share. Anyway, don't take too much. You'll be back right soon."

"You heard him. He told me I can't ever come back." Kitty picked up the flour sack and started for the ice house steps.

"Kitty?"

The sisters faced each other and Kitty saw tears in Ginger's eyes. "I'm going to miss you."

Kitty yelled back at her sister as she plunged up the steps toward the door. "Yah, you will miss having one less person to bully."

Grace met her on the road with a small package. Her eyes gleamed in triumph. "Here's some lunch for you. Be good. I'll see you one of these days."

"You're honestly going to leave, too, then?"

"Yes. I don't think my soldier man is going to come around here looking for the love of his life."

"Well, if you can figure out a way to get to Pierre, I've heard they are planning to put Army camps on Farm Island. I'm guessing you could get a civilian job in the capital city and find the perfect guy. Do you think you can convince Ginger she will be an old maid soon if she doesn't get out of here, too?"

"She knows she's letting life slip away, but she feels a loyalty to Pop and this farm you and I don't have. Twyla left because she was sent, you're leaving for adventure, I'm going to go for love. Ginger doesn't think she needs either adventure or love as much as she needs Pop's trust and security."

"Boy, what a mouthful for a little hayseed like you."

"I'm telling you truth, no more, no less. Good-bye, Kitty." Grace sent her sister off down the road with a resounding spank on the backside, then she raced back to the house.

Kitty hurried until she out of sight of the farm, then she found her feet dragging, afraid to go on, determined not to go back. She opened the packet of egg sandwiches Mom had put together from her uneaten breakfast. There, between the two sandwiches she found a note.

"Kitty, if you ever need me, I'll be here. Do not be afraid to come home. Love, Mom."

With the girl's burdens lightened, she began to hurry again. Darkness would overtake her before she could reach her destination.

She wasn't even sure how far she had to walk to reach the Williams Ranch.

A few minutes later a car pulled up and stopped beside her. A male voice called. "It isn't exactly the policy of the United States Postal Service to offer people rides, but I'll give you a lift. If you don't tell, I won't."

Kitty climbed into the car with the mailman. "I thank you."

"Running away from home?"

"If I say yes, will you make me go back?"

He chuckled. "Considering what you are running from, no. I hope you have a good place to go. Perhaps your grandmother's house in town?"

"No. She'd work me harder than Pop does or she would have me hauled back out here. I have been offered a job on the Williams Ranch."

"I would say you have found a respectable place to work. Good people, the Seversons are. Of course, they are not the owners, only managers, but they will do their best by you."

They said little more as the miles rolled past, interrupted only by an occasional stop at a mailbox.

"Well, here's the Williams Ranch road. I'll let you off here. You can walk the few miles in from the main road. Good luck, young lady."

She thanked the driver, got out and walked under the arched gateway.

As the sun drew high towards the noon mark, Kitty's body ached and she longed for a drink of water. Her feet were arguing with her shoes, so she sat down in the dirt, took off the shoes and put them in her pillow case bag. After a minute's rest, she got up and strolled on.

A bull snake lay stretched out across the road, absorbing the heat. He stared at Kitty's passing with lidless, cold eyes and made no move. Still, she gave him plenty of room.

She passed a wheat field where men were threshing. Several waved at her and the girl considered walking over to ask for a drink of water. When she did not find the recognizable figure of a certain man on the crew, she forced herself to move on down the road.

A few minutes later she heard the roar and rattle of a pickup truck behind her and turned as the vehicle pulled up beside her and Mr. Severson spoke. "Hop in if you can find a space and I'll give you a lift down to the house."

Kitty looked at the four men packed into the cab of the pickup, then her eyes searched the crowd of strong young men in the back, their tanned faces grinning at her. She looked back at Mr. Severson. "I believe I'd better just keep walking."

One young man offered from the pickup box. "There's room beside me, honey."

Kitty's face flamed.

"Not a bad day for walking, I'll agree," Mr. Severson replied in his noted-to-be-kind voice. "There may be more room on the next train through." He sent her a wink, then let the clutch out with a jerk and the pickup roared away.

Kitty puzzled over his statement as she watched the vehicle depart in a cloud of dust. She hadn't moved from her spot on the side of the road when a team pulling a wagon appeared in the distance. A few minutes later a straining team of big, black horses stopped beside her, stomping and pulling at their bits. Kitty looked up into the warm, brown eyes, which day and night had haunted her dreams for more than a year.

Brice laughed when Kitty told him about the offer to ride in the crowded pickup box.

"I would have had to stand on somebody's toes," she told him.

"Sounds like Sonny's kind of idea to make room for you by him. He thinks he's God's gift to women."

Hearing the unfamiliar phrase left the girl without words until Brice explained. "He's quite a ladies' man."

"Do you mean you wouldn't have offered to let me stand by you if you had been in the pickup?" Kitty surprised herself when she could give voice to such a daring thing and not blush every red-hued color possible.

"I would have gotten out of the pickup and let you have my place," he quipped, "or at least I would have made you the same offer Sonny did. But at least you know me and I know you."

Then after a bit of silence, he asked, "What are you doing out here walking on a hot afternoon."

"I ran away from home."

"That's been a long walk."

"I caught a ride with the mail man, but I wasn't supposed to tell that."

"Oh, government regulations? You're not the first person he has given a ride. Why did you come this way?"

"Your boss asked me to come work here. That was the day you guys brought the team to our place. I was hoping to get here before you started harvest, but I didn't have the nerve to just up and leave."

"And?"

"I prayed a lot and it seemed like God said, 'Go on, get out of here.' And here I am. I hope Mrs. Severson still needs me."

"Oh, she does. She will be glad to see you, and so will Ole. He worries about her a lot."

"You know them pretty well?"

"I would say so. I work year around for them. Most of the rest of that motley crew you saw in the pickup travel with the threshing machine."

Kitty stole a look at the young man from where she stood beside him at the front of the wagon, hanging on to keep her balance as the Blacks moved along the dusty road. She noted the sheen of sweat from the summer's midday heat and the smooth working of muscles in Brice's tanned arms as he managed the reins of the trotting team. Even though his head and the strong lines of his face were as usual, shaded by his battered straw hat, once had been enough to impress on her the memory of his straight hair, so dark brown the strands were almost black, worn short on the sides and back. She wondered if it curled on the top of his head under his hat. Kitty wished he might take both reins in one hand and reach out to draw her near to him. And she knew if he did, she would yield to his touch as if she had already spent years by his side. He was the closest thing she could imagine to a Zane Grey cowboy.

The girl shook her head as if trying to clear away some thought. Could she be awakening to the idea where her dashing young "Cowboy" came upon the scene in battered straw hat and bib overalls?

Kitty required little time to adjust to the way of life on the Williams Ranch. She rose before sunrise to have a roaring fire in the cook stove when Mrs. Severson appeared in the kitchen. She had replaced her bibs and shirts with a cotton dress, covered by a full, long apron Mae gave her.

The first morning her employer asked. "Would you like to mix the pancake batter while I get the table set?"

"I don't know how to make pancakes, ma'am," Kitty explained. "I've spent too much time with cattle to learn the fine arts of cooking, but I'll sure learn in a hurry if you'll be kind enough to tell me what to put in the bowl."

The older woman's smile made an immediate appearance on her pleasant, round face. "I will enjoy teaching you to cook. After breakfast we'll start on bread. Okay, pancakes first. Now here's the mixing bowl. Put in some flour," and popping off the lid of the metal flour can, she used a tin cup to dip out flour, which she dumped into the bowl. "Then you need a little sugar." This ingredient she poured from a glass jar.

Kitty watched wide-eyed as the other woman added baking powder and salt, measuring them into her hand. Fortunately, Kitty could count the eggs and the bacon grease was spooned into the batter, so she formed some idea how much of those ingredients were used, and she guessed one would know how much buttermilk to add to get the batter thin enough to pour.

She stared into the bowl and wondered if anything stirred together so fast could possibly taste like pancakes. But the flapjacks must have been delicious. After standing near the stove frying the cakes for close to an hour, she appreciated the cup of steaming coffee Mrs. Severson set on the nearby work table.

"Scrape out the bowl and fry yourself some cakes, Kitty. I'm going out and sit with my man a couple minutes before we tackle the dishes. Close up the stove draft all the way when you're done frying. This kitchen will be sweaty long before we start dinner." Before passing into the other room, she added, "And by the way, from now on, I am Mae to you and my man is Ole."

Kitty swabbed up the last bit of syrup from her plate with a bite of pancake just as the young man called Sonny burst in through the back doorway.

"Beautiful," he exclaimed, "I haven't seen you all morning. Have you been slaving over a hot stove while I sat out there stuffing myself? Shame on me." He uncorked a burlap-covered glass jug and poured in steaming coffee from the huge pot on the stove. Then jamming the cork in tightly, he started out the door. "We'll see your lovely face at high noon, providing the damsel ever lets the maiden out of the kitchen." The screen door slammed behind him.

Kitty stared after him, working the last of her pancake around in her speechless mouth.

When the women were washing the dishes, Kitty queried, "Where do the other men eat breakfast? I'm sure there were a lot more in the pickup then I saw at breakfast."

"Oh, several of the younger fellows travel with the thresher. And others are neighbor men who come in to help just during harvesting. My man has been gone other days helping them. And when our fields are finished, he'll be going off again to help others get their fields done. The neighbors do breakfast and supper at their own homes. We have a few extra men we hire on here during harvest. They are the ones who ate most of the pancakes you fried this morning."

Kitty nodded.

After dishes, there were chickens to kill and pick. Mae stirred up a fire under an outdoor grill where a huge kettle of water steamed. One by one Kitty picked up several roosters from a small cage where they had spent the night. She tried to be stoic as she handed the first bird to Mae, then turned her face away. She heard the ax hit the chopping block and saw the beheaded creature flopping around in the weeds. She hoped she would never have to do the killing job.

Picking feathers came next. After Mae dunked the first bird into scalding water to loosen his feathers, she handed him to Kitty. The girl finished rough-picking the big feathers and those on the breast almost before Mae handed her another bird still dripping scalding water. Her fingers smarted from the hot feathers, but she reached for the next rooster.

After the feathers were removed, the ladies "fine picked", looking for missed feathers. Mae deftly passed the carcasses through the open fire to singe off the hair so the birds were ready to be washed in the dishpan of cold water and then taken to the kitchen for gutting and cutting into eight pieces per chicken.

Kitty's experience did not include dressing chickens, or undressing them as Mae joked. Mom and Twyla always did the cutting part after the younger girls picked the feathers from the birds. Now she watched her employer clean a young rooster, and then tackled her own. Quick slashes of the knife removed legs and wings, but she cut with great caution to make an opening for removing the entrails. Since most of the noon meals would feature chicken, she assumed she would get faster at the job by the end of harvest.

Peeling potatoes came after the chicken pieces were browned and frying in big cast iron skillets. Mrs. Severson handed Kitty a dishpan. "Bring up plenty of spuds and we'll also fix a potato salad for supper."

Kitty opened the trap door the cook pointed to and walked down the steps into the dark, cool cellar. She struck a match and lit the lantern hanging near the door at the bottom of the stairs. After a few seconds, her eyes adjusted to the dim light so she could take potatoes from the bin.

Mae's voice called from above. “Bring up a couple jars of tomatoes, too.”

Kitty located the tomatoes among the rows of jars. “You sure can a lot,” she called back.

“Yes. I like to put up lots of goodies. Oh, bring up some applesauce too. Then we won't have to keep the range fired to bake a dessert for supper.”

Back upstairs Kitty peeled potatoes and chatted with the older woman while they worked.

At noon the men came from the field, their faces streaked with sweat and dirt. Mrs. Severson carried out the water bucket and the fellows dashed the dust from their faces and hands in the basin on the back porch, dumping out and refilling the container with clean water as needed.

After the women carried bowls and plates of steaming food to set on the table in the living room, the feasting began. Kitty moved here and there, filling coffee cups, slicing bread in the kitchen, and passing a pitcher of milk. Later she served pie. Sonny received his piece with a “thank you, beautiful.” The men laughed and Kitty blushed. When Brice caught her glance in his direction, amusement danced in his eyes. She hoped he was laughing with her, not at her, and responded to him with a private smile of her own.

She ate at the kitchen table, keeping an eye on the menfolk as they finished their pie and needed coffee cups refilled.

Brice came to fill a water jug at the kitchen pitcher pump. Mae chose the moment to speak to Kitty. “Sonny sure likes you.”

Kitty blushed at the mention of the young man before she saw the mischief in Mae's expression.

“Of course,” the older woman continued, “I think he knew what he was talking about when he said you were beautiful.”

Kitty slid her empty plate across the table for a piece of pie. “Hs appears to me to be a flattering liar.”

“Oh, I don't know but what he might be telling the truth,” Brice interjected, but walked out of the kitchen before either woman could answer.

Mrs. Severson gave Kitty a raised eyebrow, but the girl only shrugged while hoping her employer could not hear her pounding heart.

CHAPTER NINE

Sunday was Kitty's hardest day. All week long she had toiled beside the older lady, preparing food and washing dishes. But Sunday morning she had built up the fire in the cook stove before Mrs. Severson came into the kitchen.

"No rush today, honey. We take life easy on Sunday along with the menfolk."

Later she put on the best dress of the two she possessed and rode into town with Ole and Mae for church services. The bench was hard against her back and her feet hurt from wearing shoes, but she enjoyed the singing and preaching. She had to admit she had not been to church since she was a tiny girl.

After a dinner of cold roast beef sandwiches and garden lettuce with a cream dressing, she went upstairs to her room. Often she lingered there, enjoying the flowered wallpaper and frilly white curtains. Her bed was spread with a colorful handmade quilt. But since no cooling breeze came through the big east window, Kitty went back downstairs. Mae had retired to her room and her husband was asleep in his rocking chair.

Kitty went out through the kitchen doorway to the back porch and sat down, her legs dangling over the edge. She still wore her best dress, but the shoes were in her room.

"Shame, a big barefooted girl like you," she scolded herself. "Eighteen. It is time for you to learn to wear shoes all year around." Then she let her mind wander off and sat staring across the prairie, seeing her brown-eyed cowboy come riding down into the valley and across the meadow. So far away were her dreams she did not see or hear him coming, but there he was beside her, laying a book in her lap.

"I've heard you love to read," Brice said. "There are a few books in the bunkhouse. They are mostly westerns, but I'd guess you don't mind that."

A moment passed before the startled girl could speak. "Thank you. I was wondering what I might do all afternoon."

Brice leaned against the porch. "Would I be very out of line if I asked where you were when I walked up here?"

"Where I was?" Kitty frowned. "Oh, well, I was admiring the prairie, how the pastures stretch across the valley to meet the hills over there." She hesitated, "But I would not be honest if I left out what I was thinking of. The cattle there grazing; I do miss the cattle. Bread dough and mashed potatoes are okay, but housekeeping just doesn't have the smell and feel of a herd of cattle."

"Did you ever hear this?" and with a quick voice he recited several lines of a poem.

"I ride on over the range
With my pony and gun.
Like a drifting tumbleweed
T'ward the setting sun.
I've broken many a bronco
Branded many a steer;
But the whirr of a rattler
Still fills me with fear."

"I like the poem," Kitty exclaimed, "Who wrote it?"

"An old schoolteacher of yours, C.H. Robinson."

"Ah yes. He was my teacher when I was only five years old and Mom said later I should not have gone to school at such a young age. I can remember him holding me above the heater to warm me up when I got to school on cold days. He also let me put my head down on my desk and sleep when I felt like. And I felt like it most every day. I had to take first grade over." Kitty sighed. "Mr. Robinson was a good teacher, but I certainly didn't learn everything he tried to teach us. A poet I'll never be."

"Me neither. I'd rather sing."

"Then sing for me."

"Not right now," he demurred, looking at Sonny as he came toward them. "I'm thinking about seeing if the fish are biting. Would you like to come with me?"

"Kitty is going walking with me," Sonny stated shortly, standing before them.

Kitty gasped in silent shock and before she had a chance to argue, Brice shrugged and stalked off toward the bunkhouse. She was slow about getting to her feet as she watched him go, then she turned on Sonny, "I wouldn't go to a concert of Katydids with you." She stormed into the house and let the door slam behind her.

During supper, Kitty stayed in the kitchen. When the meal was finished she watched from the window as Brice went back to the bunkhouse. She could hear Sonny talking with Ole and she had an uneasy feeling pestering her when she started washing dishes.

When Mae picked up a towel to dry the dishes, Kitty spoke up, "I'll do the dishes alone, ma'am. I didn't help serve the table."

"But you did get most of the food ready."

"I needed something to do to keep me busy," Kitty smiled slightly, "I'd have put rocks in a couple salads if I could have been sure two certain young men would get them." She didn't care if Sonny had overheard her comment when he entered the kitchen.

"That's life," her employer chuckled, "full of rocks."

Sonny took the dishtowel from Mae. "I'll help with dishes."

When the older lady left the kitchen, Kitty did her work in miserable silence. After some time passed, Sonny spoke, his voice carrying a gentle tone. "Kitty would you walk with me tonight? The temperature is cooling down a bit outside."

Kitty's first thought was to deny him, but her second thought was of an evening alone in the big, stuffy house so she changed her mind. "You throw out the dishwater and I'll put these dishes away and we will check out the cricket's song."

She found Sonny easy to talk with as they strolled across the yard and along the edge of the shelterbelt. The young man told Kitty about his family and he included enough tales to make a book, some she could believe, others she laughed at and decided he was a tad bit windy.

For some time they sat without speaking near the creek and watched the pink and gold sunset. The strains of a guitar and voice came over the cooling evening current.

"When it's nighttime in Nevada, I'm dreaming
Of the old days on the prairie with you."

Kitty reveled for just a moment in the thrilling words of the sweet tenor, wanting more than anything to be sitting at the feet of the brown-eyed singer.

"A beautiful evening," Sonny murmured for her ears alone, "and such a beautiful girl." He reached for Kitty's hand, but she was too quick for him to catch her as she leaped to her feet and bounded away.

"Like a frightened doe," he thought as she disappeared over the creek bank.

She splashed through the water and was charging up the hill before Sonny got his legs working. He hesitated a moment at the water's edge, reluctant to soak his Sunday shoes, then made a heroic leap and cleared the creek's small stream. When he caught sight of the girl again, she was still running, her dark hair streaming back from her face.

At the top of the hill she halted and stood in awe of the glorious display of sunset colors. He joined her to watch the magnificent display until the last red sliver of sun disappeared. Dusk came without lingering.

He reached for Kitty's hand again, and again she avoided him, racing like a startled rabbit back down the hill toward the house. He caught up to her by the garden. "I'm glad I was running after you and not from you," he panted.

Her merry laugh rang through the dusk, "I might run after a horse or a coon, but never a man." The screen door banged behind her and she went giggling up the stairs to her room.

♪♪♪

She was hanging laundry on the clothesline on Monday afternoon when a car drove in to the yard. A lady to whom Kitty had been introduced at church climbed out and walked to the porch where she was greeted by Mae.

When Kitty walked into the kitchen with the empty clothes basket, Mrs. Davis and Mrs. Severson were seated at the kitchen table, waiting for water to boil for tea.

Mrs. Davis patted at her face with a hanky and Mrs. Severson suggested, “The air is much cooler in the living room, my friend. Kitty, would you bring us tea when the kettle sings? And would you make the bread dough into cinnamon rolls and set them to rise? On second thought, glasses of cool water will do for now. We will have tea when the rolls are baked.”

“Yes ma’am.” The girl was pleased Mae had taken for granted she knew how to make cinnamon rolls.

She found the job was not as easy as she had anticipated. The dough stuck to the rolling pin and then absolutely would not roll out into a big circle like her mother’s always did.

Ole came into the kitchen to fill his water jug. His shirt was soaked with sweat and grease covered his hands. “Got the threshing machine fixed,” he told Kitty as she ladled water into the glass jug he had put on the washstand. “We’ll finish up this afternoon if nothing breaks again.”

Kitty’s mind played with his words as she fussed with the bread dough. The finish of the harvest would also mean a finish of her job here. And she just wasn’t quite sure she wanted to be a maid in a hotel in town.

Ole had been watching her from the doorway. “If you keep messing with the dough, your rolls will be tougher than chicken’s feet.”

“Chicken's feet aren't tough if they are prepared right.”

“You mean you actually eat them?”

“My sister Ginger does. I've never been able to get past thinking about the places those feet have walked regardless of being scrubbed, skinned and scrubbed again.” Kitty reddened, of course. “I can’t get a nice big circle like my mom does. See how ragged the dough is?”

“So what? Roll it up and slice it straight and no one will even know it wasn’t a perfect circle, providing you eat the two end pieces.” Mr. Severson smiled and departed.

Kitty looked after him, “Now I wish I had some common sense like him.” She followed his instructions and soon had a beautiful roll of cinnamon and sugar-sprinkled dough ready for slicing.

In a baking pan she spread brown sugar. Then she poured cream over the sugar, stirred the mixture together and laid the roll slices in the syrup. While the rolls were rising beside Mae's smooth loaves of bread, Kitty carried out the wash water and brought in dry clothes from the line.

While she folded laundry, she kept humming parts of a melody she had heard Brice singing. She had the notion the young man was unhappy about her going for a walk with Sonny. "What was I supposed to do," she muttered, "sit around like an old maid?"

After the dough had risen to double the original size, the big pan of rolls was put into the oven to bake. Then Kitty stepped out on the porch, hoping to coax a small breeze to stir the damp curls away from her neck. But the day was still, the heat choking. She could hear the threshing machine in the field and saw belches of black smoke rising straight up into the sky as there seemed to be no currents to carry the exhaust away from the field.

"Finished tonight," she sighed. The idea of leaving the Williams Ranch and the comfortable big house did not appeal to her at all.

While the rolls were cooling, she made tea. Then carrying a plate of rolls, cups and the teapot, she made her way to the living room.

Mrs. Davis ceased talking the moment Kitty stepped into the room. After a moment of uncomfortable silence, Mae began to talk about the heat.

Kitty's face burned, her ears burned, her neck burned. She trembled as she put the tea and rolls on the table near the women. But as she turned to flee, Mae spoke to her.

"Why Kitty, what a lovely topping on the rolls. What is the recipe?"

Kitty turned in surprise. "Nothing but brown sugar and cream in the bottom of the pan. You bake the rolls in it. Mom always makes the caramel using cream and brown sugar."

"Your mother is an excellent cook," Mrs. Davis stated. "She always used to take home the blue ribbons. But I haven't seen her at the fair in years."

Kitty turned away, speaking as she went. "She's always too busy." The mention of her mother had brought quick tears to Kitty's eyes, and a heaviness pressed against her chest. She knew the ladies had been talking about her. What had she done to cause gossip? Mom would be so ashamed of her. She returned to folding clothes, snapping and smoothing out wrinkles from the towels, pressing out ridges from the socks with her fingers and collecting a large pile of clothes to be dampened for ironing. All the while she attempted to imagine what had caused the ladies to talk about her. Maybe she should wear shoes. Maybe they were amazed that she had only two dresses to wear and neither fit her well. Maybe she should not have gone walking with Sonny.

When Mrs. Davis prepared to depart, she stepped into the kitchen. "Thank you for the tea and delicious rolls."

Mae paused at the screen door before accompanying her guest to the car. "Kitty, please believe me. We weren't saying anything bad about you. We were … well, we were planning a little surprise for you." Then she hurried down the walk to say goodbye to her friend.

After the car drove away in a cloud of dust, Mae hurried back toward the house and called across the porch. "Let's bring in the rest of the clothes from the line, Kitty. There's a storm building."

Kitty ran outside with a basket and they wasted no time gathering clothes from the lines, pitching the clothespins right in with the fabric. They could be sorted out later.

"We'll finish drying these in the kitchen. But just as soon as we get them into the house we'll take dishpans and pails to the garden. I have a feeling those ugly clouds are carrying hail."

"Pick off all the beans and peas," she told Kitty a few minutes later. "I'll get the tomatoes and corn. We'll have to can all we can yet today and hope to finish tomorrow."

Dark clouds rolled, gathered and swirled in the southwestern sky. A straining team of horses came into the yard with a wagon load of grain. They dashed into the barn, where the team was unhitched and a tarp spread over the wagon box to help keep out any rain trying to sneak through the barn roof.

The truck was brought in and unloaded, and then returned to the field.

When the wind made a screeching appearance, Mae and Kitty hurried about the house, closing windows against the dust. In the yard, dirt and trash flew high and swirled. The women paced from one window to the next, checking for tornado clouds.

The truck came again and this time was also driven into the barn. Ole made a run for the house, but the rain and hail caught him at the gate. Kitty held the screen door open as he staggered into the room. Then she securely latched the outside door and closed the heavy inside door against the storm.

They watched as wind and rain lashed out in fury. Branches snapped from the trees and crashed against the house. Water seeped in around the window sills and had to be mopped up with rags. Hail beat against the west side of the house, then the wind changed directions and the hail beat the paint off the north side.

Suddenly, with the same fierce speed the storm had come, the tempest blew out and was gone.

The mud squished between Kitty's toes when she trudged outside to survey the damage. All the chickens had fled to safety in their coop, but were coming out to strut about the yard, stopping to sip a drink from a puddle, but not daring to step into the water.

The garden resembled a parade of toy soldiers with bare stalks stripped of leaves and produce. Kitty surveyed the sad mess from the garden gate, wriggling her toes in the gooey mire.

A teasing song came to her ears.

"I traced her little footprints in the mud,
I traced her little footprints in the mud,
God bless the happy day, When Kitty lost her way
And I traced her little footprints in the mud."

Kitty faced Brice. "You know he traced her footprints in the snow and her name was Nellie."

"Is that right?" Brice paused and studied the girl a moment, laughter in his eyes. "I suppose I really should have sung, 'I traced her number nines in the mire.' Right?"

Kitty snorted, "Size five and one-half, smartie." Then she giggled as she lashed out to kick a shower of mud from her foot, spattering him.

Before she could run, the young man swept her up in his arms and carried her across the yard, "See that big, big puddle?"

Kitty saw and screeched. Closer and closer the muddy water loomed at her. The girl squirmed, then clung desperately to Brice, her arms tight around his neck and face pressed close against him. "If I go into the puddle, you're coming, too."

"Not if…I can get your arms loose," he panted, working to loosen her grip. Then he teased, whispering in her ear. "The shame, hugging me right out here in broad daylight."

Kitty gasped and her hold slackened, "I'm not hugging. I'm hanging on for dear life."

"Feels like hugging to me," he was still whispering and his face was very close to Kitty's. He held her a moment longer, then let her stand on her feet. "Now run, before I rub your nose in the mud."

She ran, and found Mr. Severson and his wife standing on the porch, laughing.

The trio headed for the garden to rescue whatever vegetables they could. They carried pails and dishpans of produce into the kitchen.

A short time later Brice joined the couple and Kitty as they worked. "Thought I'd help you all get some of this produce in the canner," he stated as he scrubbed his hands at the wash stand. Then he put a paring knife to good use.

With the extra helping hands, the group soon had all the usable vegetables packed into sterile fruit jars and steaming in the canners on the cook stove.

"Feels like a sweat shop in here," remarked Mae. "But is sure is good to have the garden stuff taken care of. The temp is cooling down outside. Let's get out there as soon as we can."

Since the rain had been brief and hard, the dirt road leading towards town was packed hard. Sonny and the other hands still at the farm packed into a pickup and headed off for whatever reason. Kitty didn't inquire.

At dusk the lamps were lit only for washing dishes. Mae sent Brice to the bunkhouse for his guitar while she and Kitty made quick work of tidying the kitchen.

They gathered out on the porch in the damp coolness of the evening. Brice's guitar and sweet tenor voice carried them through the miles of time, from Foster's "Oh, Susanna" and "Beautiful Dreamer" to "Roundup Time in Texas" and "Nighttime in Nevada."

Soon Mae rose from her chair on the porch and motioned her husband to follow. Kitty was alone with the man and his guitar and the star bright South Dakota night.

His voice crooned on.

"I hear a mockingbird, down in the little green valley,
He's singing out his heart to welcome me.
There she waits by the garden gate down in the little green valley,
When I get home again how happy she will be."

When the song was finished, he rested the guitar on his lap and they talked, first about horses and cattle and the prairie.

When he was quiet she wondered what he was thinking of. Finally, he leaned back against a porch post. "I once traveled north and east of Van Metre. You know where Van Metre is?"

"Sort of. Your sister and her family live near there, right?"

"Yes. Actually we drove on past Van Metre. Over near where my brother-in-law grew up, there are no bridges over the river. If it is high, you have to walk across the railroad bridge. When Bad River is dry or low, you cross it by fording it."

"Fording? Like driving a Ford through it?"

"Not exactly," his smile was warm. "Crossing a stream of water on rocky ground so the tires don't sink in or the wheels if you are driving horses pulling a wagon."

"Okay. And?"

"To get from Van Metre to Wendte, you have to ford Bad River twice. There are bridges over Bad River the rest of the way to Fort Pierre."

"Why aren't there bridges between Van Metre and Wendte?"

"That's a good question." He picked idly at the guitar strings. "Probably because there isn't enough demand for a good road between Van Metre and Wendte. You can go up the hill from Van Metre, across the prairie and back down to the river. That's where I saw my little green valley. It's at the end of the road if you are traveling up the Bad River from Fort Pierre and do not want to cross the fords."

"Sing it again. The song about your little green valley."

"There's only one thing ever gives me consolation.
And that's the dream that I'll be going back some day.
At night down on my knees, I pray the Lord to please take me.
Back to that little green valley far away."

When the song ended, she noted the sadness in his brown eyes.

He sighed. "It's a nice dream, but I am a poor man. In the hard years, my father lost nearly all his land right along with most of our neighbors, but he chose to stay on while the others left."

"Where did they go?"

"California, Oregon, Washington mainly."

"I'm glad you and your family did not go away."

He didn't hesitate. "Good thing, huh? And I guess I can keep dreaming. One never knows what God has in store for those who trust in Him."

He trailed his fingers across the strings. "This one is for you, m'lady."

"Shine on, Shine on, Prairie Moon, Up in the sky,
I ain't had no lovin' since January, February, June or July.
Dark time ain't a good time to spoon
So, Shine on, Shine on, Prairie Moon,
For me and my gal.

When he left her with a quick peck on her cheek, she glowed with happiness as he disappeared into the darkening night.

Several days later the Seversons prepared to make a trip east to Presho. Kitty knew they were intending to retire eventually to that area and agreed with Mae that she could manage the kitchen in the older lady's absence.

She was chopping vegetables to add to a simmering beef broth when a timid knock sounded at the screen door.

She looked up to see her little brother waiting outside. "Teddy, how did you get here? Surely you didn't ride horse all the way here on such a hot day."

He followed her into the kitchen and sat down near the work table. She filled a glass with lemonade from the ice box and set it in front of him.

"Daddy dropped me off out at the mailbox on his way to Draper. Not so far to walk. I told him you would figure out a way to bring me home in a few days. Where's your feller?"

"Cleaning up a mess. One of the guys on the haying crew hooked a rake in the barbed wire fence."

"Seems to me they ought to clean up their own mess. I'll bet there is fence to fix, too."

"Well, unless you want to help me make dinner, maybe you can just take your little self out there and offer Brice a hand."

"Little? I'm almost as tall as you."

"But not quite. And even if you were, that would not be much to brag about."

He drained the glass, shrugged and went outside to see if he could locate Brice.

Brice. Ever since his quick peck in the dark, she had wondered what it meant. It sure didn't feel like what she had read about in Ginger's romance magazines, nor in any Zane Grey novel. She sure hadn't seen flashing lights and rainbows and felt breathless. She figured it must have been a token of friendship and she had better get her head out of the clouds and concentrate on her work.

Besides Teddy, Brice and another hired man called Tom, the haying crew polished off every crumb of food she set before them including the beef stew, biscuits and apple crisp with whipped cream to top it. They washed it all down with coffee and vacated the house.

She looked at the mountain of dishes and groaned. "Maybe I should call in the dog and let him lick the plates. I bet no one would ever know if I put them away in the cupboard." She giggled as she piled the plates in the hot, soapy dishwater.

The day had cooled very little with the passing of the sun.

Thankful that Ole had recently brought fruit from the store, she whipped more cream, sweetened it and added chopped apples and bananas. Together with sandwiches made from leftover beef roast, she presented supper to a much smaller gang of diners.

The haying crew had gone to their home, so Tom, Teddy and Brice were her only guests. Tom and Teddy helped wash dishes and clean the kitchen while Brice went out to do the evening milking and gather eggs.

It was nearly dark when he came to the house with his guitar. The group sat around on the porch and listened, sometimes joining in on a song.

When he eventually laid the guitar to one side, and Kitty had sent Teddy upstairs to sleep. Tom took the hint and strolled off towards the bunkhouse.

Kitty turned toward Brice, who was now standing, having laid down the guitar. He pulled her gently into his arms. "Let's see if we can do this better." He kissed her lips, softly, lingering only a moment before he stepped back. "Do you mind?"

She hesitated, "I guess it depends what it means. I-I haven't had much practice."

"Am I the first man, then, to kiss you?"

"I'm nodding, but I think you cannot see that in the dark."

"I like that. I hope you can keep it that way, but there's Bob and George and Sonny. A feller could get jealous real easy with all those guys around a very pretty girl."

She had thought Brice was a man of few words.

He reached for her again. "Once more, then I'm heading for my pillow."

His kiss lasted a bit longer than before.

She watched him fade into the shadows and wondered just exactly what was going on.

In the days that followed, he barely talked to her. Frank and Twyla picked up Teddy and took him home. The haying was finished except for hauling the stacks in closer to the buildings. Bob helped Brice roll wagonload after wagonload of hay up into the mow of the barn.

She was cleaning up in the kitchen after breakfast when Brice came in from outside, toting the cream separator parts. He set them on the work table. "I'll heat up some hot water and give these a good cleaning."

He glanced around the kitchen, but seeing no one else present, he stepped up to her, wrapped her in his arms and kissed her so soundly her world spun.

He heard Mae's footsteps coming toward the kitchen door, and stepped back.

Obviously, he was a bit shy.

CHAPTER TEN

Fair time. The pumpkins lay like huge golden balls among the drying foliage of gardens. Frost had come and the green leaves of summer had taken on an autumn splendor.

Kitty shivered as she climbed the hotel stairs. Although the daily heat penetrated the interior of the big inn, the girl felt a lonesome foreboding.

She was thankful to the Seversons for gaining a position for her in the respectable hotel, but making other people's beds and picking up after them was by all means not her favorite activity. As for carrying out chamber pots, well… "I'd rather be cleaning the chicken coop," she noted in her diary.

At home Mom would be canning pumpkin and putting up the last of the pickles. Soon she would start butchering old hens and packing them into jars for canning. Then during the winter, there would be steaming bowls of dumplings and chicken. Although thankful for a job and opportunity to earn and save a bit of money, Kitty often longed for country fields and open land.

"Best hurry, Kitty," her employer called up the stairs. "The judging should be done by ten this morning. You will want to go see which ladies took all the blue ribbons."

Kitty looked back, puzzled.

Her employer laughed, "I guess I forgot to tell you. The rest of the day is yours. There are only the four rooms you've already been working on. But I expect a crowd will be moving in tonight. However, fair time is for us, too. Today we'll do no more around here than is absolutely necessary."

Kitty sped through her chores and was finishing the last room when her employer's voice rang up the staircase again. "You have company, Kitty."

In the lobby she found Mae Severson holding a dress box tied shut with a lavender ribbon. "Here's your surprise, Kitty. I bought the fabric, Mrs. Davis sewed it and we thought you might like to have it for the harvest festival dance tomorrow night."

The girl was awed to silence. With trembling fingers she took away the ribbon and lifted the lid from the box. In the folds of tissue lay a dress, sewn from crisp white poplin with tiny, green leaves scattered about it. The neckline featured a standup collar accented by green satin ribbon to tie in a bow with the ends curling down below her waist. The puffed sleeves were gathered just below the elbow. Yards of material made up the billowing skirt. Mae took another green, satin ribbon from the box.

"For your hair."

"I…I don't know what to say," Kitty's lips trembled.

"Then don't say anything. Only if you're still footloose and fancy free come next harvest, we'd sure love to have you come help us again. However I have an idea you'll be keeping your own house by then."

A sneaky blush crawled right up her neck and across her face. Even her ears burned.

Mae continued, a smile playing at her mouth, "Of course, you'll have to make up your mind which one. The young storekeeper over in

Draper said this fabric looked lovely against your face. He suggested the green ribbon for your hair."

"Storekeeper?" Kitty echoed. "Of all the nerve. He did hold this very same fabric up by my face. Embarrassed the blush right out of me. But he's certainly not my boyfriend. Not even a friend. I met him one time when I went in the store to get groceries for Mom. He was absolutely rude. And, he's Ginger's boyfriend."

"Not to listen to him, he isn't." Mae started for the door. "Well, the judging of home goods ought to be done by now. Your boss lady says you might want to ride over to the fairgrounds with us if your cleaning is finished."

"Oh, yes. I just have to make up the last bed. I'll only be a minute."

"I'll be happy to wait for you. The mister always goes off to look at the hogs and horses. I'll enjoy the women's exhibits much more with another gal along. Join us outside when you're finished."

Kitty hurried to finish the room, called to her employer to say she was leaving, then after slipping off her apron, she ran outside to join the older couple. Oh, yes, she did put on her shoes.

The endless rows of needlework and culinary temptations greeted their eyes at the women's building. Kitty marveled at the countless, tiny stitches in the crocheted pieces. "My chain stitch will never amount to something like this."

"It's not hard to pick up the other pattern stitches. Oh, what a lovely quilt."

Kitty read the name on the display tag. "My grandmother."

"Beautiful work, and all hand stitched."

"I suppose she wouldn't have one of those newfangled sewing machines," Kitty mused.

"Newfangled?"

"Well, to her they are still newfangled." She pointed to a cape made of many different colors of yarn. "Is this knitting?"

"Yes. And this is tatted." Mae hesitated before changing the subject. "Tell me something, Kitty. I sense the relationship between you and your grandmother is not what it should be."

"I visit her once in a while."

"Because you want to or because you feel it's your duty."

"How did you know?"

Mae shrugged. "I don't honestly know, but honey, life is too short not to be on good terms with your grandmother. Loved ones who have lived long and well, have a lot to contribute on how to succeed in life. "

"I suppose you're right." They were walking towards the foods section.

"Do you want to talk about it?"

Kitty sighed, "You know my Daddy died a couple months before I was born."

"So I have heard, and…?"

"His mother and his two sisters wanted to split up my three older sisters amongst themselves and send Mom and 'the brat' back to Mom's family in Montana."

"The brat being yourself?"

"Exactly." Kitty was staring at row after row of jars of sparkling jellies and jams in an array of color. "Even though my grandmother did not get her way, I find it very hard to forgive. If they had been there to help Mom instead of hurt her, she probably would not have married the first man who proposed to her."

"There is also a story where your daddy asked this man to look after your mom and your sisters."

"So I've been told. Maybe I believe it, maybe not. And I suppose Pop felt divorcing his wife and marrying my mother was the way to do it. But you know, he also got a nice ranch thrown into the deal."

"I understand your bitterness," Mae sympathized. "But if possible, you need to let it go. Forgive as the Heavenly Father has forgiven you."

"I've tried to, many times." She swiped at the moisture sliding down her cheeks.

Mae handed her a hanky. "Don't quit trying. Make an effort to be friends with your grandmother and your aunts. Ask Jesus to love them through you, even if you can't stand them. Gradually, the forgiveness will come."

They moved down the aisle between rows of goodies. "Oh look," exclaimed the older lady. "It looks like your sister Twyla is stepping into your mother's shoes." She touched the blue ribbon on a golden loaf of bread.

"Here's some little jars of jelly she made, too."

The sun had moved past its high noon place when the two women left the building. Kitty ate sandwiches with her friends near their car. Then Ole invited her to join them in viewing the afternoon's races.

They sat high in the grandstand and enjoyed the foot races and children's pony races. Then the tracks were cleared of children and spectators as the teams were brought out for buggy racing. Kitty immediately sought out a certain beautiful black team. They were pulling a lightweight, single seater carriage.

"I brought my bride home in that buggy," Ole mused.

"With the mothers of that team pulling it," Mae added. "And do you think they'd stand so he could help me out? No ma'am. I had to jump quickly and not get caught between the wheels if they broke away."

"So," questioned Kitty, "are you telling me this team actually belongs to you rather than the Williams Ranch?"

"Yes, it does. This team will stay with us as long as we are able to work. Hopefully we never have to sell them to buy groceries."

A titter weaved through the crowd when a mismatched team moved on to the track. The one horse was a mottled gray, standing very tall and was very skinny with ribs plainly showing. His teammate was a short legged, fat roan. The two-wheeled contraption they were pulling appeared to be a last minute idea.

"I've seen them race before," Ole commented. "They may well run away with first prize."

And he was right. When the racers came into the final stretch, the strange team was running neck and neck with the blacks. They crossed the finish line just ahead of Ole's beautiful team.

Mae snorted, "They wouldn't have beat our team if they'd had to pull anything heavier than a tin can. And look, their driver is half the size of Brice."

Her husband chuckled, "How much did you bet on the race, Mama? You're not losing very nicely."

She snorted again, "Well, if I were a gambling woman I would have lost a great deal. I should have gone visiting rather than sit here at a horse race and steam."

Ole stood. "Let's go down to the track, Kitty. You need a ride in my old buggy."

Drivers were cooling their teams as the pair made their way amongst them toward the blacks. Brice pulled up the team. "Sorry, boss."

"Did your best. We couldn't expect to beat any team while pulling a…a…"

"Tin can?" Kitty teased.

"Oh, you women. Slide over Brice and give this little gal a ride in my old buggy." Ole handed her up into the vehicle. "Make my team step pretty now. They aren't even blowing. Guess they didn't realize the race had even started. No wonder they got beat."

Ole led the way to the gate and allowed the team and buggy to pass through before closing it.

They drove in silence away from the fairgrounds and skirted the town. Kitty began to have the pressing fear Brice resented her riding with him, but she could not fathom why he would feel offended. What had happened to the guy who kissed her so soundly the last chance he had?

At last she broke the silence. "What time would you say it is?"

The young man tilted his head to glance at the position of the sun. "Four, four-thirty."

"I suppose I must be getting back soon. I have to work tonight."

"I can leave you off at the hotel unless you have to go back to the fairgrounds."

"I don't have to go back if you will tell the Seversons where you left me so they won't worry."

He nodded.

Silence again. Then they were trotting up Main Street, avoiding slow moving motor cars and pedestrians. A flush rose in Kitty's cheeks as people turned to look at them and many smiled or even waved.

Before the hotel he stepped out and helped her down from the buggy.

"Thank you for the ride. The horses are beautiful."

"My pleasure, miss," he nodded and she thought he was about to say something more, but then he didn't, so she stepped up on the porch and watched him drive away. With a wondering, sad ache in her middle, she went back to work. She could not imagine what had happened to the carefree hours they had spent at the farm. What had happened to make him so quietly serious? Was he devastated about losing the race? Had there been money involved somehow? Or, was he resenting her willingness to allow kisses without any word of marriage? She swiped away quick tears, pasted on a smile and went inside the hotel.

She was caught up for a time in the gaiety of the hotel's guests as they dined. But when the work was finished and she was in her room alone, the heaviness again pressed upon her. She raised the window and sat in darkness, listening to the sounds of the night. People laughed in the street below. In the distance the calliope from the traveling carnival played merry tunes.

"I think I'll just go home. "Pop must be over being angry by now. I'll go home and eat Mom's good cooking and have my sisters to talk to. I'll ride Bronco, and…and…" Kitty slammed her fist against her palm. "And clean barns and build fence for the rest of my life for a man who cares for no one but himself? I will not."

She prepared for bed without lighting the lamp, and brushed her hair until the sparks from it flickered in the darkness.

"There's so much I want to do. What's to stop me, really? Always, I've wanted to fly." She twirled about the bedroom with arms spread wide. "And I shall write a book and travel a great deal. I will see Alaska, and Hawaii, maybe even Holland."

So Kitty dreamed of the things she wanted to do in life, but as she slipped away to uneasy sleep, a handsome face and warm, brown eyes pressed in visions before her.

Early morning found her back at work. Every room in the hotel had been occupied and when Kitty had at last finished her cleaning, it was mid-afternoon and she was very tired. Without stopping for something to eat she went to her room and slept until her boss called her to serve supper.

On this night, the hotel's female guests appeared in lovely dresses for the harvest festival dance, and Kitty's spirits ebbed even deeper. When the dishes were washed, she joined the old folks lounging on the porch.

The sounds of the fairgrounds drifted across the night. Laughter, occasional shouts and the music; Kitty separated the accordion from the violin and the violin from the guitars, then they blended again with the stomping of feet on the bowery.

Her employer appeared in the doorway, "Kitty, aren't you going?"

The girl shrugged, "I don't think it would be proper for a young lady to go out there alone. And I'm rather tired."

Old Sam never missed a beat in his rocking, "I'd be glad to see you to the dance, Lassie if I was able. Ya know that, doncha?"

She leaned over and kissed the weathered cheek. "I'll bet you set the girls a twirling in the old days, didn't ya."

"Only one, Lassie. We started loving each other in first grade and never strayed. But, why don't you go put on this fancy dress I heard about and show it to us old duffers."

"Yes," her employer encouraged. "How about the dress? Surely you won't disappoint the ladies who made it by not wearing it."

Kitty looked down at her work-reddened hands, "Oh, there will be another time, I expect."

"Just the same, you get yourself upstairs. I've drawn a fragrant bath for you, and if nothing else, you can relax in it and daydream about the good-looking feller I saw you with yesterday."

She had to agree the bath was luxurious. The big clock in the hallway struck ten just after she had toweled off and slipped into a clean everyday dress. She went down to sit on the porch and once again enjoy the evening. Sam evidently had taken himself off to bed and the other old men had moved off through the darkness to their homes. The last couple went into the hotel for a cup of tea before retiring. Kitty wondered if she could find nerve enough to go alone to the fairgrounds.

She was still standing by the door trying to make up her mind when a motor car stopped before the hotel. She recognized it even as Frank stepped out and came up to the porch. She stepped forward and took his proffered hand.

"Good evening, miss. How does it happen we find you here and not out dancing with the other maidens?"

"I'm afraid of the dark," she whispered, sharing his good humor. "I hear the music. You could come up here on the porch and dance with me."

"Or maybe not." He dropped his voice so no one else could hear, "I was asked to see you to the Harvest Festival."

"You were asked?" Kitty queried, a puzzled little frown creasing her forehead. "But why didn't..." she hesitated, wondering just what she should say.

"Your sister says for you to get your hair combed. Now."

Twyla's voice came from the car, "And wash your ears."

Kitty laughed, "Both of them?"

"Absolutely."

"I'll be only a minute."

"Here." Frank handed her a narrow package tied shut with a strip of rawhide. "He said this was for you."

While she searched for words to question Twyla's man, he shrugged and turned away.

She then fairly flew up the stairs to her room and with shaking hands put on the lovely new dress. The green bow was set jauntily in her brown tresses.

She hesitated only a moment before snatching the package from her bed and tearing away the leather strip and wrapping paper. A pair of shiny black patent leather flats tumbled on to the bed. They had big taffeta bows over the toes. And they were a perfect size five and one/half. For a second she remembered the day she had kicked mud on him.

Frank whistled at her when she stepped out on the porch and then he helped her down the steps and into the car beside Twyla.

At the fairgrounds they parked the car and made their way to the bowery.

"I should have known," Kitty breathed. The strum of one of the guitars came to her through the night in a familiar sweet song. She dared not lift her eyes to the beloved face of her favorite guitar picker.

Frank spoke, "Since I have you here, I will repeat, I was sent for you. You can see why he couldn't come for you himself."

She nodded, afraid to look for her voice.

The crowd pressed around the bowery to watch the graceful dancers. The long-time-married couples were easy to pick out, their steps perfectly matched, moving in blended rhythm. Kitty's foot tapped with the music.

A drunken man staggered up the steps of the bowery, leading a straggle-haired woman, and they stumbled about among the other dancers. Kitty drew back from the platform, sharp distaste fading out the lovely music.

Frank shook his head and spoke to her. "I'm sorry. It's people like that who give the dance its bad name. They drink and stagger, and by midnight some of them will cause fights. Then the non-drinking people go home in disgust and on Sunday morning the preachers shout against the sins of dancing."

"They need Jesus," she whispered.

"Yes, but at the moment they wouldn't listen if you did try to talk to them."

After a few more round dances, the music changed and a thin old man in overalls and a fancy striped shirt stood up to call for groups of four couples to join hands for square dancing. The couples paired off in two to a set to follow the commands of the caller. Three couples stood off to a side of the bowery, searching for a fourth to complete their square. When one of the dancers caught Frank's notice, he glanced at Twyla, who nodded and patted her bulky, with-child, front side. Frank swung Kitty up on the bowery, then he joined her and she was whirled through the steps of the square dance.

"I don't know how," she panted as she was handed from one man to the next in an "Allemande left, right, promenade home and swing. First couple out and peek, back to the kitchen and swing."

Her heart pounded with the clapping hands and stomping feet. She was confused, but found if she relaxed, she could enjoy herself as skillful hands guided her through the swinging dance steps.

After several sets, the music changed again. Smooth ripples of the "Blue Danube" moved gently across the bowery and the couples melted into the even swing of the waltz. An accordion picked up the plaintive melody as Kitty stepped back to the edge of the dance floor and watched Frank dance with his bulky little wife with such tenderness, she ached in happiness.

Even so, she stood uncertainly on the bowery, wishing she could disappear into the darkness of the night. But then strong, warm arms moved her into the swaying dancers. The crowd pressed them close together and his lips moved against her hair. "I love you, Kitty."

One guitarist was missing from the band.

They stood still in the middle of the bowery, the others couples moving around them. His hands touched her hair and tilted her face to look at him. He saw a veil of mist in her eyes as he drew her tenderly to himself.

Once again the tune changed, and he sang for her ears only.

"Let me call you sweetheart, Darling, I love you.
Let me hear you whisper, That you love me, too."

"I love you, too." She whispered.

He hugged her close. "I am a poor man. I tried to fight the feeling I have for you, but I cannot. Yesterday I had decided I was not being fair to you to let you have hope for us. Tonight I know I do not want to go on without you. I prayed you would come when I sent Frank to get you."

"But the shoes…"

"I saw them in the Mercantile. They were dusty and the clerk made me a good deal. They were too fancy for a child and too little for a fancy lady, but just right for my girl."

"I promise I won't wear them in the mud."

CHAPTER ELEVEN

Business at the hotel slowed enough after the Harvest Festival to shorten Kitty's hours and income. She was thankful her work paid just a bit more than for room and board at the hotel.

Twyla's baby was born in October. The frost was still heavy in the morning sunshine when Frank stopped at the hotel to tell Kitty the news.

When it was finally time for her noon lunch break, she withdrew a few dollars from her saving envelope, put on a sweater and walked down Main Street to the Mercantile.

Choosing a gift from the display was difficult. Kitty touched the dainty booties and sweaters and caps. She admired the coats, bonnets and dresses. At last she picked out a little pink dress with tiny ribbon bows. The clerk wrapped it in fancy tissue paper for no extra charge.

On the way to Mrs. Morgan's home she noted an advertisement in a window of the theatre. The door of the building was locked, but she made a mental note to come back during the evening hours. Another job would help her savings grow and she might even get to see the movies for free after she sold tickets to folks.

At the midwife's big house, Twyla welcomed her with a warm hug. She unwrapped the layers of tissue and exclaimed her thankfulness over the gift. Kitty leaned over the big buggy and touched a tiny rosy cheek. The baby roused, stretched and yawned, then went back to sleep. When she touched the baby's hand, her tiny fingers curled around Kitty's digit.

"Seen Brice lately?"

Kitty shook her head before answering. "Not since the fair. I think he doesn't come to town very often." She sat down in the only chair in the room, hoping that was why she had not seen him.

"He doesn't have a car. I would guess the lack of anything to drive other than horses hinders his courting."

"Who is he courting?" Kitty smirked.

"Well, if not you, then you are both quite fickle. And shameless! Hugging on the bowery, no less," Twyla teased in return.

"We were dancing."

"You weren't moving one little toe, sister. Tell me, have you made any plans?"

"Nothing new. I don't care much for working at the hotel. I'm about ready to roam, but I don't know where I'd go even I had extra money. You know I always wanted to see some country besides the prairie. But I did notice an ad for a ticket clerk at the theatre. I think I would like that job and forget about traveling."

"And you would do well at it, you being so friendly and all. And I'm sure you can count change properly. But I meant have you and Brice made any plans?"

Kitty shook her head without hesitation and changed the subject. "Have you been home lately?"

"Right after the fair. Everyone there is fine. They finished the fence. Mom got all the garden stuff canned. It just doesn't seem the same as when we lived there."

"I suppose not. I guess we would not turn back the hands on the clock even if we could. I don't even remember life being so great when we were little girls."

"I don't suppose it was. We never went hungry, and Pop always made sure we had a new pair of bib overalls and a couple shirts once a year. He even let Mom sew us a new dress every couple years."

"Yes, once or twice we even got new dresses from the Montgomery Ward catalog."

They sat in silence for a while. Kitty studied the pictures on the walls.

Some pickle-faced woman dressed all in white stopped in the doorway. "Little girl, you need to be going home now so this new mother can get some badly-needed rest."

Kitty looked around her as if wondering who was being addressed.

"There is no one else here. We must limit visits to one person at a time and then only for a few minutes. She sniffed loudly. Kitty shrugged, got up and pulled on her sweater.

"Come back after supper." Her oldest sister requested as she made a face at the retreating woman. I pay for my room here. I can say who can visit and how long you can stay."

"She'll be off duty by then and the night help is much more pleasant."

"When do you plan to escape?"

"Ten days. Ten days of lying in this bed, and I'll bet I won't be able to walk when I do get up. These baby doctors could take a good lesson from our Indian friends. They don't lie around like they just had major surgery."

She shrugged and departed. On the street she checked, and found the theatre door still locked on her way back to the hotel and then again when she returned to Mrs. Morgan's after supper.

Twyla was nursing her baby when Kitty slipped quietly into the room and parked herself on the only chair in the room. She listened for the sounds in the house or even of the night, but the huge house lay quite still in the darkness.

"Are you the only one here?"

"There are two other mothers with babies."

"They sure are quiet."

"For now. It's not late enough. Both babies start howling around midnight," Twyla said. "But they quiet down pretty quickly once they start feeding."

Footsteps sounded in the hallway. Frank and his brother appeared in the doorway. Kitty was quick to look away and despised the flush creeping up her face. Then she forced herself to look up, whisper "howdy" and smile, just for him.

Frank sat down on the bed near Twyla and picked up her hand. Brice leaned over the buggy to admire the baby, then straightened and glanced around the room.

"Guess you'll have to sit on the bed by me," offered Frank.

"No. I see a chair for me." He helped Kitty up from her place, sat down and pulled her on to his lap. Then he put his arms around her and hugged her close.

Twyla laughed. "So, you were just dancing the other night, huh? Looks to me like you've had some practice hugging."

"Who needs practice. Comes naturally, I think."

A few minutes later Brice slid Kitty off his lap and stood up. "Will you excuse us, please? I came to town to see the girls. And since I've had a good look at the little girl and her mama, I'll take the big girl out walking in the moonlight, if she will go." When he looked at Kitty, her affirmative nod came without hesitation.

"Well, I don't know," Twyla remarked, aiming a question at Frank. "Do you suppose we should let them go out in the dark alone?"

They didn't wait to see if he would pretend to argue. Out beneath the upside down bowl of a diamond-studded sky, he drew her close and laced his fingers with hers. "I'm sorry I haven't gotten to town to see you before this."

"I had begun to doubt your love."

He stopped walking, looked down and saw her mischievous grin. "I was hoping you were joking, because doubting my love is something I hope you never have reason to do." He started off again and continued talking, "Ole and Mae send their best wishes to you."

"Oh. Give them mine when you return."

"I won't be returning to the Williams Ranch for some time, maybe not at all. There is a chance I may be able to rent a small place on White Clay Creek near where Frank and Twyla live. Anyway, I'm going home tonight to help Dad and Frank for a while. My parents are planning a trip to the west coast where they will spend the rest of the fall and winter, possibly spring. So Frank can use an extra hand."

"I see," she agreed, "but you are headed back towards the hotel. Are you taking me home so soon?"

"Yes. Little girls ought to be sleeping by now."

"They are."

He squeezed her hand. "You're a little girl. My little girl."

"Getting rather possessive, aren't you?"

"Yes." He walked her up the steps of the hotel and down the long porch to the shadows of the north side. Then he located a chair and with gentle hands pulled her down to sit on his lap.

The porch was vacant except for the two of them. When Kitty shivered, he wrapped his jacket around her, and held her close. "Frank will be coming for me soon." His voice was soft, like the starlight. "The midwife will be running him off lest he tire the new little mother."

"Beautiful baby," she murmured, allowing her head to rest against the warmth of his chest. She could hear the steady thump of his heart.

"They all look the same to me."

"I suppose, so I guess they are all beautiful."

Somewhere inside the hotel a door banged. Kitty tensed. Then the screen door opened and her employer stepped out and glanced around. "I thought I heard someone out here."

"It's just me."

"Alone, Kitty?"

"No ma'am. Brice is here with me."

"Oh, all right. How's the new baby?"

"A darling."

"Of course." She went back into the hotel and the screen door clicked shut.

Kitty relaxed against Brice. The silence of the night was sweet to her ears.

A car drove around the corner and chugged by with enough racket to wake sleeping dogs. Several put up a howl.

"I'm glad the car wasn't Frank's," he spoke against her hair. "I don't want this moment to end so soon."

"When are you coming back?"

"I don't know. Maybe Sunday afternoon. Frank will be coming to visit Twyla and the baby. Will I be able to see you then?"

"If you wish."

"Oh yes, I wish. I do so truly wish. I wish for much." He gave her a quick squeeze. "Kitty," his voice lowered to a whisper. "Marry me."

He didn't ask if she would. He just told her to do it. Her breath caught and quivered. "When?"

"Tomorrow."

"Tomorrow?" she echoed.

"Well, tonight, if sooner would be better, but I don't know if a wedding can be arranged on such short notice. A preacher might need a little bit more time, and I don't think the midwife will let Twyla out of bed, even for something so important as our wedding. I suppose you would like her to be there."

She giggled, in spite of herself.

"What's so funny?"

"Nothing. It's just...well, it's so sudden or something." She slid off his lap and he rose to stand beside her.

"Sudden?" he questioned. "I've loved you so long, little darling. Maybe since I first saw you out in the pasture with mud in your hair, or it might have been the day we went fishing for bullheads or when I traced your little footprints in the mud. I just never felt I could tell you before the night at the harvest festival." He caught her hands in his. "Tell me, Kitty, do you really, truly love me or were you just answering the song?"

"I'll have to think about it." She let a moment of silence pass between them. "Okay. I've thought about it. If this isn't love, I wouldn't know what else to call it."

"Then marry me."

"I want to, but I have nothing to bring into this marriage. I have no cattle, no horses, no land, nothing but the shirt on my back, and not many of them." She slipped off his lap and stepped over to stand at the edge of the porch. "And there's so much I want to do before I settle down. I'd like to see some country, maybe even learn to fly an airplane."

"Another Amelia Earhart?"

"No. She disappeared last July. But she did write a book, too, and I'd like to write a book."

When he said nothing, she went on. "I'm confused. What do I really want?"

He was standing very close to her as Frank's car pulled up before the hotel. "It's okay, Kitty. I shouldn't have brought it up when there was so little time to talk about it. Don't worry over it. We'll discuss the idea on Sunday." He squeezed her hand, slipped down the porch steps and climbed into the car where he cranked down the window and waved to her as they drove away.

Kitty's steps were slow as she moved into the hotel, her heart tearing at her thoughts while quick tears formed in her eyes.

Her employer came down the stairs to meet her as she struggled to make herself go up. "You better catch your fine young man before Uncle Sam gets him."

"Uncle Sam?" she hesitated. "What does he have to do with it?"

"War is building again, dear. Japan is picking on China. Germany is up to no good. And we know the United States won't stay out of it. Your young man is prime age for the draft."

Kitty made it inside the door of her room before the tears came in an uncontrollable rush.

♪ ♪ ♪

The days dragged by in long hours toward Sunday. Kitty felt as slow as the passing of time. She lingered outside when she shook rugs, wishing life could be simple and she could be back with Bronco herding cattle. She caught herself thinking with her hands resting on the dishpan instead of cleaning the plates and cups. Brice had said not to think about his proposal, but she could think of little else.

When she went to visit Twyla and the baby, she sat in silence until her sister asked whatever was wrong.

Her answer was a surprising question. "Why did you marry Frank?"

"He was a guy. The only guy. And he asked me to marry him."

"And you fell in love with him right away?"

"I suppose."

"Why?"

"Because he is so nice." Twyla lifted the baby to her shoulder and softly patted her back, urging the production of a noisy little burp. "Why are you asking me this?"

"Well," Kitty stared at the picture on the wall above Twyla's bed. "I'm wondering if I had the chance to get married, would I?"

"Would you or could you or should you?"

"All three, I guess."

"Well, I suppose you could. There's no one to stop you, anyway, not legally. And you would if you had a mind to. But should you? Depends."

Kitty's stubbornness flared. "Depends on what?"

"Do you have anything in common with the young man?" Twyla quoted a verse of scripture, "Can two walk together except they be agreed?"

Kitty sprang to her feet. "Oh, it isn't any fault in him. We have much in common. No, I'm not worried about him. There could never be anyone else for me. But I'm not sure I'm ready to settle in one spot yet. And what if he doesn't want to wait for me until I grow up? There are so many things I always wanted to do before I got married. So did you, if I remember right. There were all sorts of things you wanted to do. What happened to them?"

Twyla shrugged. "They lost their importance as Frank grew dearer to me, I guess. By the time he asked me to marry him, I only wanted to make a home for him and the children we might have."

Kitty glanced at the buggy and a tingle of joy swelled over her. "You aren't going to need any outside excitement for a few years, I'd say, what with this little miss around."

"You are right. I'm thinking I will have all the excitement I need for at least 21 years or so. Actually, I'll probably never be bored again. Mom told me 'once a mother, always a mother, whether 20 or 40 or 60 years pass by, you never completely let go.'" She handed off the sleeping baby to Kitty who cuddled her a moment, then tucked her into the buggy. "But Kitty, why worry about this until he asks you. Or did he?"

For a moment, Kitty reflected on her sister's smiling countenance, then answered. "Yes." She fled the room.

Friday evening, when she knew the theatre would be open she went back to inquire about the job, hoping the position had not already been filled.

The owner, who was busy selling tickets, replied, "Step right in here, young lady and try your hand."

In spite of her anxious nerves, she calculated prices for three singles, one couple and two families, counted back change and handed out tickets.

"You're hired. And when the rush slows down, feel free to watch the show. I can see the front door from the popcorn stand."

"Seventh Heaven," starring Janet Gaynor and Charles Farrell, was the first free movie she watched.

On Sunday, Frank waited in the car while Brice went into the hotel lobby to call for Kitty. The younger brother was wearing his Sunday best corduroy slacks and a white button down shirt. He carried his jacket folded over his arm.

Kitty had robed herself in the green print dress with its green ribbon curling below her waist and the other green ribbon nestled in her brown curls.

He whistled under his breath and caught her hands in his. She was afraid he was about to kiss her in front of everyone in the hotel lobby.

"Winter's coming," he said instead and put his jacket about her shoulders.

They rode with Frank to the midwife's home where the older brother got out, then Brice got into the driver's place and the Model A chugged off down the street and out across the railroad tracks toward the fairgrounds.

In the silence, Kitty noted the barren trees, stripped of their last golden leaves. She saw the weathered buildings of the fairgrounds.

Brice parked the car near the place where the bowery had stood. "When you were seventeen I talked to you here. I carved a trinket of wood for you and even then I wanted so much to put 'I love you' on it. It was the only way I could describe how I felt about you even back then."

"I still have it," she whispered.

He continued, "When you were eighteen I finally dared to tell you of my feelings. Will you marry me when you are nineteen?"

"In March?"

He nodded, "I am not a man who speaks many words, Kitty. Neither am I a writer of fancy phrases as are my parents. I do know poetry, but at the moment 'Still sits the schoolhouse by the road, a ragged beggar sunning, around it still the sumachs grow and blackberry vines are running' doesn't seem really appropriate."

"Your mother tried to get me to learn those lines when she was my teacher in school. I didn't do much with it, but I do remember parts of this one. 'School days, school days, dear old golden rule days, Reading and writing, and 'rithmetic, taught to the tune of a hickory stick. I was your gal in calico, You were my dashing, barefoot beau, I wrote on your slate, 'I love you, Joe' when we were a couple of kids.'"

"Joe is the mailman. Do you really love him?" He teased.

"There is only one man I love." She pulled away from him, but only far enough to allow her to meet his eyes.

"Your dad?"

"I never knew him. He died three months before I was born."

His smile disappeared. "I'm sorry. I did not realize he had been gone so long."

"I'd like to meet him some day. Twyla said he was tall, strong, quiet and before he died he told her she should love Jesus with all her heart so she could be with him in heaven some day." She then moved back into the close comfort of Brice's arms. After a few long minutes, she encouraged him, "but you were saying…"

"Somehow it doesn't seem important now, but I suppose my words are necessary. I don't have much to offer you. Right now all it can be is a rented house and barn on a few acres of rented land with little or no money to buy things we need, even groceries to eat. Some day maybe we can own a ranch in a little green valley with a herd of cattle grazing and horses on the hills, but for now…"

When he hesitated, she inserted, "It's you and me and a dream."

He mused. "Sounds like the words to some song." His brown eyes searched her face.

"I'll be nineteen on the fifth of March. Shall it be on my birthday, then?" Kitty's lips quivered.

"If you will."

"I will," she whispered.

Then his face came close and his lips brushed hers, then settled in to be more demanding. "Now I'm going to catch up on a few of those times I wanted to kiss you and didn't dare."

"I think if you had dared, I would not have resisted."

"Do you mean you loved me as much as I loved you way back then?"

"I suppose I have loved you for a long time, but I didn't realize it. And I was afraid Ginger was going to steal you before I had a chance to see if I could catch your attention."

"Never." His lips seemed to taste hers, then they swept her crashing down into a world she had not known existed outside of the Zane Grey novels she had read. Blues and reds and golds swirled around her and it wasn't at all like those books. It was deeper, more beautiful, more meaningful.

"Payback for the day I carried you in the mud," he whispered.

"If this is what I get for being naughty, I'm going to make a habit of kicking mud on you." This time Kitty leaned against him, whispering just before she claimed his lips. "This is for the night you first asked me to marry you."

Then it was his turn. "This is for the time we all went fishing."

"You wouldn't have dared way back then."

"Way back then. You were sitting there by the dam and at last you looked at me." Brice's eyes sparkled with love and mischief. "Only then I was not sure about the love part. There you were with your hair flying and wearing your faded old flannel shirt and a pair of baggy britches held up with binder twine. And you were barefoot. I just thought I'd sure like to kiss you just to see what you would do, but of course I would not have taken the chance of someone getting mad at me, including you."

"H-m-m."

He did not give her time to think of an answer. And after a few more remembrances he didn't say anything.

"Run out of reasons for smooching with me?" she teased.

"Who needs a reason?" Again he swept her up into heady clouds.

They got out of the car and walked in the crisp fall air, silently enjoying each other's company until it was time for her to head for the theatre to sell tickets.

"If you and Frank come to the movie and sit in the back row, I can come sit with you as soon as about everybody has bought their tickets."

"What's showing?"

"It's 'Married Before Breakfast.'"

"Who's in it?"

"Robert Young and June Clayworth. My boss said the movie was just released this year. I'm amazed that we can get that new of movies out here on the prairie."

"Ah, these modern times."

They drove back into town. After picking Frank up from the midwife's home, they ate supper at the hotel, then she hurried down the street to her job at the theatre's ticket counter. Frank and Brice's offer to wash up supper dishes for Kitty's boss was accepted and greatly appreciated.

Still, they were at the theatre before the show started. They held a seat for her in the back row while the crowd of movie patrons was ticketed and seated. Soon she brought a box of popcorn and the three enjoyed the movie.

As they began the walk back to the hotel, Frank stated, "You two take your time. I'll go warm up the car."

"Thanks, brother," Brice replied, leading his sweetheart into the shadow of a building.

"A kiss to last a week, at least." He murmured. "I don't know when I can get back to town."

She ventured, "I wanted so much for you to kiss me the night of the fair. But now I'm glad you waited until I promised to be your missus. Oh! How I love you."

He sang softly against her hair.

"Just you and me and a dream
And a love that will not die.
We'll meet the world hand in hand
And conquer all by and by."

CHAPTER TWELVE

On the first Sunday in November, they filled out an order to Sears and Roebuck for her wedding dress, rings and a tablecloth.

He had showed up at the hotel in time for supper, so helped clean up and wash dishes afterward. When they left for the theatre she noted a strange car parked outside the hotel.

"My folks had some family business to attend to in Washington, so they left their car in my care."

"Washington? Do they get to see President Roosevelt?"

"Nope. Other direction. This is the state of Washington. Mom's sister and her husband had shares in a mine out by Cle Elum. And I have an uncle and cousins in Oregon, so they will be spending some time with them, also."

"They went by train?"

"Yup."

On the way to Frank and Twlya's place they pulled off the road and spent some time kissing.

After church the next day, and Sunday dinner, they did some shopping by catalog.

That next Saturday night Brice waited for her until the theatre crowd had dwindled and she was free to leave. Her boss handed her two quarters, her regular wage for the evening's work and waved her toward the door. "Go have a good time, kids."

They drove north of Murdo to Van Metre. It was time to dance. She knew there would be other Van Metre dances where she would be alone while he played in the band, but tonight she had him to herself. Except, of course, when she had to share him with all the gals who knew what a great dancer he was.

She wished Frank was there to dance with her. But it would not have been right for him to come when his wife was resting up from producing a baby. Ole asked her to dance a few times, and that was fun until she remembered how jealous Brice had been about Ole buying her basket at a social. It wasn't her fault her favorite guy was off picking corn for some farmer at the time, now was it? And the basket social was for the benefit of the local school YCL.

Still, she had fun. Brice went up to the stage and spoke to the lead musician, then he came to her, reaching for her hand.

"I'm going to teach you how to schottiesch."

"How to what?"

"It's a type of polka. I'll walk you through the skips and turns a couple times before they actually play the music for it."

So, she learned to schottiesch. The music was perfect, and after twice around the hall she was following his pattern, and loving it. She hardly noticed when other dancers cleared to the sides of the hall and gave them the floor for their intricate dance. And if she had not already loved him, she would have by the time the music ended.

♪ ♪ ♪

Her engagement ring was a diamond chip set in white gold basket weave. He chose a lovely Indian Summer day to give it to her.

It was her day off from work at the hotel, so he came early in the morning to take her to the country in Frank's car.

"Let's start this day right," he said as soon as they were in the car. Then lifting her hand, he slipped the ring on the right finger of her left hand.

Speechless, she tilted her head to receive his kiss.

"We will make this a day to remember," he told her. "Frank and Twyla are expecting us for dinner."

"Do they know?"

"About us? They cannot help but know we are in love. You can tell them the date we've set when you show off your ring."

The Model A chugged uphill and down, traveling north to leave the little town behind.

"I hope you won't mind living in the country."

She gasped in surprise before she realized he was teasing. "I will be so glad to get out of town."

"You want out so bad you'd even marry me to do it, huh?"

"Yup." She hesitated, "Brice, I know you ordered two rings, but I thought one would be my wedding ring and the other would be yours. I don't understand an…an engaging ring."

He held her hand for a moment. "Engagement. It shows the world you are mine until we actually have the ceremony that makes it so. I hope you don't mind that I probably should have saved the money to buy groceries."

"I trust you to know what you are doing, sweetheart. I will wear it until death parts us. Is that out of some book?"

"It's part of the marriage ceremony."

"H-m-m. I like that. Tell me more."

"I don't know it all. Something like, for better, for worse, in sickness and in health, for richer or poorer...that's the part I'm worried about. How can you still love me when there might be nothing to eat but dandelion greens?"

"Believe me. I was not born with a silver spoon in my mouth. Mom worries that when Teddy grows up the women will be after him because he has a ranch. I, however, will do well to come to you with the shirt on my back."

"And I might be able to keep a faded dress on your clothes hanger.

"Try me."

"I plan to."

Then Brice indicated a dust cloud far up the road. "I'd say the H Bar H cowboys are moving cattle home for the winter. They rent summer pasture over this way somewhere."

"I should think they're big enough without renting land."

"Seems to be the richer a man gets, the more he wants."

"Then let's not get rich."

"We are already rich. We have each other." He squeezed her hand. "But as far as material goods goes, we won't have much to worry about for a while, maybe never. You have agreed to marry a man who is poor by the world's standards."

"I'd rather have a poor man's dandelions than a rich man's gold." She hesitated, "Are those lines from some song, too?"

"Maybe, maybe not. Anyway, we can make up a tune for it and sing it. We'll make our own song."

"I can't sing."

"I would guess you actually can. We will have to work on deciding for sure. But even if you cannot, I have enough music in me for both of us." He let go of her hand as the car slowed down to approach a milling herd of cows and nearly-grown calves. He shifted down to low gear and moved carefully through the rippling mass of white-faced red cattle. Cowboys on splendid horses weaved back and forth, urging stragglers, their whoops and "git along" hollers ringing in the crisp morning air. Several of the men lifted hands in acknowledgment of the couple in the car.

A lump pressed at Kitty's throat as the familiar bawling and stomping brought quick tears of memory and let one or two slip down her cheeks.

"Wouldn't it be something to have this many cattle?" he asked.

"Dreamer."

"Well, you and me and a dream."

"Sure is enough to get started with."

"We'll be living on love."

"Yup. Got plenty of that."

The lead group of cattle parted to let them pass through their midst. A cowboy wearing a bright blue shirt with a red scarf about his neck whipped off his hat and bowed low over his saddle in her direction. Kitty was sure she saw him wink at her.

"I've always heard my folks talk about keeping the wolf away from the door. Somehow I don't think they were talking about what I'm thinking."

Her only response was a puzzled look. Then a few minutes later they drove up to a tiny, tar-papered, square house which was home to his brother, her sister, and their baby girl.

Brice walked hand in hand with her across the yard. "Frank is in the barn, so I'll let you go in to your sister." He squeezed her hand and headed toward the corral. Kitty drew a deep breath and turned the knob on the door of the little house.

In the spotless kitchen area, Twyla was finishing the preparation of pumpkin pies. The golden sauce was flecked with cinnamon and cloves and corralled by high crust edges. She dusted the excess flour from her hands and hugged Kitty, then exclaimed over the ring.

"I thought you might have something to show me today. Have you picked a date for the wedding?"

"My birthday."

"What a special birthday your nineteenth will be, baby sister. It is hard to imagine you are so close to twenty. Why, you are almost an old maid," she sparkled.

"Which makes my older sisters, Ginger and Grace, old maids, I suppose?"

"Of course."

Twyla's baby stirred in a cradle, which began to rock with her movement.

"Where did you find this beautiful bed for your baby?"

"Frank made it. He didn't even have a pattern."

"Wow." Kitty sat down in the nearby rocking chair, then reached to trace the delicate carvings of the cradle with her fingertips. Then she brushed the soft curls around the baby's itty bitty ears.

"I reckon I'll be loaning you our cradle in a year or so."

Kitty's hand jerked back to her side as she turned to face Twyla. "Oh no. I'm too young to have a baby."

Her sister's laugh was warm. "Then you'd better not get married, little sister. These things happen, you know. Remember our old rhyme? 'First comes love, then comes marriage, then comes Kitty with the baby carriage.' Life happens."

A tiny tremble edged through Kitty. She had never really considered what it took to make a mother. What if she didn't qualify for such a demanding job?

"Spoofy will outgrow the cradle before we know it."

"Spoofy?"

Twyla twinkled, "Brice's name for her. He seems to always have a nickname for people he loves."

"I probably don't want to know mine." Kitty watched Twyla put the pies in the oven, musing over what she saw. Pretty, neat, efficient, the older sister was making good use of the skills she had learned at home under Mom's patient teaching. There was a spotless cloth spread on the table, bright curtains at the windows and a shine on the cook stove. Kitty looked down at her work-reddened hands. A gal doesn't learn much about homemaking by spending her life in books and pastures, or cleaning hotel rooms.

The nearby baby stirred again, blinked several times, stretched and yawned, then stared at Kitty with her large, blue eyes.

When she whimpered, Kitty rocked the cradle gently, but the whimpering grew louder.

"Suppose you let me peel spuds. You come take care of your little human."

"You'll need the practice."

Kitty got to her feet. "First of all, you let me learn how to keep house and take care of a man. We'll take the rest when it comes."

"You mean 'when *they* come,'" Twyla retorted and carried the baby off to the bedroom to change her diaper.

"Surprised she didn't make me do the stinky part," she muttered as she paused at a window to drink in the beauty of the autumn day. The ring felt heavy on her hand. She tilted it in the sunlight until the diamond caught the sparkle and cast tiny rainbows on the wall.

Then she went to the kitchen table and peeled potatoes. Twyla came back to sit in the rocker and nurse her baby.

"Tell me something, sis."

When Twyla looked up, she continued. "Brice said something about keeping the wolf away from the door. What does he mean?"

"U-m-m. Hunger, maybe? Where or when did he say that?"

"We had been talking about being rich with dandelions is better than a rich man's gold."

"But you still have the wolf by the door. Maybe it comes from the story of the big bad wolf who was always trying to have three little pigs for dinner."

"Maybe. Kinda funny, though. We were driving through the H Bar H herd and this good looking dude cowboy winked at me. I thought that might have been the wolf Brice was referring to."

"Jealous already? You know, little sister, you are a friendly person. People like you. They are drawn to you. Take my advice and be really careful not to do anything that will make your man jealous."

"Not even checkers with Theodore at the hotel?"

"Is he ninety years old and half-blind?"

She giggled. "Not exactly."

"Then you might be better off staying in your room crocheting."

She sighed. "Boring."

"Yup. And safe."

Kitty heard the creek of the rocker, her sister's humming, the teakettle singing on the back of the stove and her own heart calling for peace. For once the lump in her throat was from pure happiness.

All too soon the meal was over, dishes done and it was time for the happy couple to get back in the car and drive the mile over the hill to the southeast to where they would be making their home in a few short months.

The house where Kitty would come as a bride huddled in the shelter of rolling hills and a winding tree-lined creek. A large, faded red barn, a weathered chicken coop and what appeared to be a falling-apart shelter for hogs stood near each other across the yard from the house. A tipsy pen made from Cottonwood logs might keep in hogs or it might not. The corrals seemed to be in better shape than the fence, which sagged around the house yard.

Brice pushed open the rickety gate at the end of a weed-edged dirt path leading to the porch of the house. "No one has lived here for years, but I think the house is in pretty good shape."

The porch was not a porch as far as Kitty was concerned. It was a type of platform or floor, built close to the ground, running perhaps eight feet wide and as long as the front of the house. Close to the front edge a tall pitcher pump appeared to have survived time.

"I might have to put new leathers in the pump." We will hope the cistern under it still holds water." Brice stepped up to the door where he produced a skeleton key and fitted it in the lock.

Upon opening another door in the small entry way, they stepped into a big kitchen. Cobwebs and a general musty smell greeted them.

"Oh!" She exclaimed, "a cook stove. Does it work?"

"I don't know. I hope so."

Kitty peered behind the stove. "Do you suppose these mice will share the wood box with us?"

Brice leaned across the range and saw the round nest made among chewed corn cobs and a few wood shavings. "How do you know it's a mouse house? Maybe it's a rat's home."

Kitty's nose wrinkled in distaste. "It'll be him or me, but both of us won't live in the same kitchen."

"Whatever it is, the nest looks vacant. He has probably gone south for the winter."

"Mice do not go south for the winter," she sassed.

"Well, he has gone somewhere. He would be frozen stiff if he had stayed here in the house."

A door squeaked and groaned when she opened it to reveal a small pantry with sagging shelves. Brice told her he would turn the boards over and soon the shelves would be reasonably straight to hold the cans of food they would need if they figured on eating anything but milk and eggs before summer.

Lord willing, before the next fall she would load the shelves with jars of garden stuff and wild fruit from the creek if the year was good for producing plums, currants, chokecherries and buffalo berries. A shot from Brice's oil can would take care of the noise coming from the door hinges.

The other big room on the first floor had one window on the east side and another facing south. Once cleaned, the glass of the windows would let in sunshine to help take the chill from winter days.

Brice studied the room for a moment, "We will have to find some sort of heater to put in here so we can keep warm while you sit over here and knit and I pick a song on the guitar."

"I don't know how to knit."

"Well, whatever you do on long winter nights, then."

"I play checkers. One cannot play checkers with oneself." She appeared to be studying the situation. But if you play checkers with me, you can't play the guitar and I'd rather have the music than the checker game. So I will sit and look at you instead. I do know how to embroider a bit, and I can crochet a nice edge on a pillow slip, but I would rather just look at you."

"Oh you would, would you?" He tugged her into his arms, but then gently kissed the tip of her nose. "Looking at me could get pretty old."

"Maybe after a century or so." She pointed over his shoulder. "Where does this doorway lead to?"

"Upstairs, I suppose. Let's go look."

Kitty drew back and shivered. "I've never liked to go upstairs in empty houses. I don't like downstairses either."

"Downstairses? Are you sure my mother taught you your grammar?" He shrugged and drew her along, "Come on. I'll protect my little Goldilocks from the big, bad wolf."

"My locks are not golden." Laughing at her own foolishness, she followed him up the stairs. "And I was only in third grade when she taught me. How could I remember my grammar from that far back."

He opened a door to the right of the stairway. "This room would probably be best for us unless March is really cold, then we will want to temporarily have our bedroom downstairs in the living room. This south side will be the warmest in winter otherwise and there are three windows to pick up breezes on hot, summer nights."

Kitty gave the old iron bedstead a hefty shake. "If this is any good, it's one thing we won't have to beg, borrow or steal."

Brice joined her and also rocked the frame. The springs creaked and groaned. "It'll do, with some fixing."

"Sounds worse than the pantry door. Maybe you can oil it also."

An old sewing machine cabinet proved to be empty of the sewing head, for which Kitty was disappointed, but when Brice inspected it he nodded his approval, but did not give her a clue as to what he was thinking.

"We could stand some new wallpaper next summer if we can afford it," Kitty remarked.

Brice sighed, then joined her at the window facing south toward the road. "I don't feel it's fair to you, Kitty, asking you to come here. I just don't have much to offer.

Her hand touched his own, "Brice, do you love me?"

He looked down at her, his brown eyes troubled. "You know, I do, but love is not the point. You can't live on love alone. You can't eat love, you don't wear it. It doesn't buy medicine or mittens."

"You and me and a dream. You have a milk cow, right? So. there will be milk for us to drink and make pancakes and skim off the cream to go on the pancakes with a little brown sugar and we can make butter from the extra cream. We might be able to sell cream or butter or trade for groceries. We can find a few chickens to live in that run-down, falling apart coop. They should give us eggs and then chicken with noodles when they decide they won't lay hen fruit any more. Surely at least one will get broody and we can set her on some eggs to get new chickens. In the springtime we can find greens and then I'll grow a big garden and we'll get fat and lazy."

"You don't sound like a girl who just came through the worst of the Dirty Thirties."

She winced. "Pray God we never again have years like those."

He nodded. "Little dreamer, you have big plans for us."

"I'm in love. I'm in love. I'm in love with a wonderful guy." She sang the line as best as she could as she twirled around the room, raising dust. "Is that from some movie?"

"Not one that I know of." He caught and hugged her close. "Let's get out of here before I grab a broom and start sweeping the place."

"It would just get dirty again before March. Now I'd like to see the barn."

He led her across the yard toward the big, faded building. "About that milk cow. You do understand that she is just a heifer, but we are pretty sure she is carrying a calf. She is half Jersey, so even though she won't give a lot of milk with a first calf, there ought to be plenty for us to have milk to drink and cream for butter."

In the corral she noted a team of horses, not exactly a matched pair, but appearing sturdy. They both came to the fence to greet the humans. Kitty reached over the top rail of the fence to pat each velvety nose. “Now who are these fellows, and where did they come from?”

“One is a gal rather than a fellow. We call her Beauty and she is quite old, but appears to be with colt. The guy here is called John. He's young, but when he is in harness with the old gal, they can pull a hay wagon.”

“I didn't know you had a team of your own.”

“I don't, but when Ole and Mae discovered we would be setting up housekeeping on our own, they presented this rather odd combination of equines to us for a wedding present.”

She couldn't help the tears in her eyes. “A gift from the heart, and so useful.”

“Right. I brought them here last night, but I don’t figure on paying rent until we actually move in, so I’ll take them up to my folks’ place until then.”

When he opened the barn door, she stepped inside. Sunlight streaming through a glassless window lit up the motes and other particles afloat in the winter air. She climbed a ladder to peek into the loft and called down to Brice.

“Did you know there is still some hay up here? It must be old, but since it has been inside out of the weather, I’ll bet our milk cow and your team will still enjoy it.”

“That is good. I hauled a short jag of hay over on the rack when I brought the horses, but it won’t last a long time.

As she climbed back down the ladder, she remarked, “This barn reminds me of the one at home. Along the sides of the loft floor are openings just big enough to push down hay into the pens below. Those holes sure make feeding easier if one has hay in the loft.”

“Sure does. How much hay would you estimate is up there?”

“H-m-m,” she pondered, “I’d guess nearly enough to get the three of our critters through this season until there is green grass for them.”

“Great. Ready to go?”

Once again in the yard he pointed in a northwesterly direction.

"Frank and Twyla's place is less than a mile away, just over the hill to the northwest, if you go by way of how the crow flies. Our kids will be able to walk over there to play with their kids."

Wide-eyed, she paused, picturing a little boy holding a little girl's hand, walking through a pasture of yellow clover, headed for Auntie Twyla's house. After a quick shake of her head, she followed her Beloved to the car.

♪ ♪ ♪

On a clear morning in December when frost had gilded the outdoors in glitter, Kitty stepped out on the hotel balcony to shake rugs. She sucked in the cold air and shivered.

Earlier the sunrise had been a mass of pink and gold flames in the feathery eastern clouds. "How beautiful are thy creations, Oh Lord," she whispered. "I'd sing Mom's old song about coming to the garden here and now if I knew no one would hear me." Instead, she whistled the tune and snapped rugs until dust scattered and floated towards the alley below.

She was still in the midst of her morning cleaning when her employer's voice called her downstairs.

In the lobby she found a small woman, clad in an expensive fur coat with a matching hat. She was standing because sitting was too unusual a thing for her to do before at least mid-afternoon.

Kitty would never forget overhearing Pop's comment when he found Mom sitting down in the kitchen on a hot August afternoon. "Kate, don't you have anything to do?"

Kitty had been in the pantry looking for a snack to take with her to the pasture. At Pop's step in the porch she had made sure she stayed hidden until he left the house. As well as she knew his tempestuous moods, she was still shocked that he would crab at the hardest-working member of the family.

Before going back outside, she approached her mother in the parlor where she was slowly dusting the same furniture she had dusted earlier in the day. The girl gave her mother a quick hug, whispered, "You are the best," then hurried outside before her temper exposed the rage she felt.

Now Kitty tugged the older woman into her arms, unable to prevent the tears veiling her eyes and choking her throat.

"Mom, whatever brings you to town?" she quizzed when at last she could speak.

"I thought I could do a bit of Christmas shopping while the weather is still favorable."

"Great idea. I wish Christmas came at least four times a year, than you could come to town more often. Come to the kitchen. You surely have time for a cup of coffee. It's hot."

"I brought you a winter coat and scarf. It's lying there on the chair." Her mother indicated a package wrapped in brown paper. "I also brought you something for your hope chest. Is it okay to leave it in here?"

"Yes, I'm sure it will be okay. But why did you bring anything? Bringing yourself is so much more than I expected." Knowing she would receive no answer, Kitty led the way to the warm kitchen where sweet and savory smells broadcast a delightful supper in the making.

"Be careful," she warned the cook as she poured coffee for herself and her mother. "This gal doesn't know what it is to sit and watch someone else make pie."

"Kitty!"

"Well, it's true, Mom," Kitty growled as she stirred cream and sugar into her coffee.

"That is extravagant, and will make you fat."

"What? Oh, this?" she indicated the coffee. "Yes, I suppose. But I can't stand the stuff any other way." Serious lines drew the laughter from her face. "I suppose as it was in the time of war, there will be a day again when we can't afford sugar. But then we won't be able to buy coffee either. About the time I learn to enjoy the stuff, I probably won't be able to afford it."

She changed the subject. "Did you get my letter, Mom? Do you know about…" she gulped, "about Brice and me?"

A gentle nod. "Yes, I received your letter, but we already knew. We went to Twyla's house for Thanksgiving and she couldn't restrain herself from sharing such exciting news."

"You're kidding me. You got Pop to go somewhere for dinner other than some cafe when he's in town by himself for some reason?"

"Yes, he drove us there. Of course a cloud came up before we could get the dishes all washed up and we had to hurry home while the weather was still nice."

"It is amazing you even got him to go." After a pause she asked, "Will you come to my house next Thanksgiving?"

"Perhaps, but I don't know. What if you cannot afford coffee and sugar?" Mom's eyes teased.

"We'll serve you some love. We have lots of it. And we hope to have chickens and some hogs by then. I'll fix bacon and eggs for Thanksgiving dinner."

"Sounds wonderful." Mom sighed. "You know, your daddy and I had very little to call our own when we started out. And suddenly there were three little girls and another on the way. And then..." her eyes averted to the wide-eyed cook.

Kitty stirred the coffee in her cup until it whirled and almost spilled. She gulped it down. "Let's go upstairs. I'll show you where I work."

Her mother declined. "Pop is meeting me at the grocery store. I must get there soon."

Kitty's spirits thudded to her shoes. "Oh, I wish you could stay for a long time."

"I see you are wearing an engagement ring."

Kitty held out her hand for Mom's inspection and wondered if Mom would approve of such an unnecessary expense. Her Mom gently squeezed her hand. "I'm glad Brice worked extra hard to buy you something so special. Soon you will put the other ring with that one and when he is gone somewhere earning groceries for your table, you can admire the rings and thank God for a good man."

"I was afraid you were going to criticize and say it is a waste of money."

"When a gift is given, do not question it. Just enjoy it."

In the lobby, the little mother pulled on her gloves. Her lips trembled. "If I don't see you again before your birthday, Kitty, best wishes, and I'll be praying for you…and Brice."

Kitty fiddled with the frill on her cleaning apron. "Do I," she hesitated, "do I dare come home yet?"

A faint smile from her mother showed a twinge of regret, perhaps even sorrow. "Remember the song I taught you so long ago?" She began to sing softly, "*I have a fella, I have, Mama. I have a fella, I have, ha ha. I have a fella, I have, Mama, but don't you tell Pa 'cause he won't like it at all.*" The older woman's arms tugged her youngest daughter close.

Kitty nodded, her load beginning to lighten as her mother added. "When you can sing the last verse, come on home."

Kitty responded, "*And now we are married, we are, Mama, and now we are married, we are, ha ha, and now we are married we are, Mama, and you can tell Pa 'cause he can't help it at all.*"

They giggled together. Mom made one more statement before stepping out the door. "I need to get rid of a few of my pullets since my chicken house is quite crowded. I'd appreciate it if you would stop up to the farm and get them before the end of March. I'm sure I can find a rooster to send along, too. You will need a rooster if you plan on increasing your flock." She smiled and swept daintily from the hotel lobby. Kitty got a grip on her trembling lips and watched her mother move proudly down the street in the December morning.

"I forgot to thank her for the present," she sobbed inwardly. "All the times she tried to thump the idea into my thick head to always be thankful, and who do I forget to say thank you to?" Then clutching her package, she fled upstairs and threw herself into finishing the morning's tasks.

It was early afternoon before she had all the rooms cleaned and the laundry was freeze drying on the line outside. She rubbed bag balm into her reddened hands and held them over the hot water radiator in her room. When the grease had evaporated, she carefully untied the grocery string from the brown paper package. She took away the wrapping to reveal several pieces of fabric.

Three coarse fabric feed sacks had been bleached to remove the brand name, then split and hemmed to make six dish towels for the bride's kitchen. The other pieces were flour sacks Mom had saved for the youngest daughter. Their gay little prints would make kitchen curtains or pillow covers or…

Kitty closed her eyes tightly shut and wondered how many depression-age babies had worn flour sack diapers and dresses.

♪♪♪

A few days later she made her way across town to pay a long overdue visit. Her grandmother's house was a small, white frame building on the east side of town, directly across from the high school, which sat upon a hill and frowned down at country girls who had not been allowed to attend school past the eighth grade.

Kitty was unaware of what might have been her lot had she been allowed to live in this house and continue her education past eighth grade. Even now, the late afternoon winter sun failed to warm her fingers, but she did not care.

At her grandmother's call to "Come in," she stepped inside the door of the little house where her feet were cushioned by a large rag rug of many colors assembled by the little old German lady's skillful hands. Other rugs were scattered about the room and she could see a quilt in the making on a frame in the corner of the parlor. Other folks might call it a living room, but here it was a parlor.

The grandmother herself was tiny and bent with age, but her sharp, dark eyes judged anyone she pleased from behind wire-rimmed glasses.

"So, you're going to get married," she stated bluntly. "Seems like girls these days just don't know when they are well off."

"Have they ever?" Kitty asked, unbuttoning the new coat her mother had brought a few days before. She laid it over the back of a rocker, which had cushions of embroidered velvet pillows.

"I suppose not," the grandmother replied, measuring coffee into the pot and setting it over the hottest part of the stove. She took a loaf from the bread box and cut two generous slices, which she set on the round kitchen table with a ball of butter on a small cut glass plate and a small jar of preserves.

While waiting for the coffee to boil, Kitty studied the large framed pictures on the parlor walls; pictures she remembered hanging in their same places even in her youngest childhood. There was a faded reproduction of Da Vinci's "Last Supper", an oval portrait of her grandfather, a picture of Christ with an exposed heart, which Kitty had never understood and wasn't about to inquire of her grandmother now.

Next to that was the striking appearance of the handsome, solemn man who had fathered her sisters and herself before his untimely passing, the man her mother had loved more than all else.

The grandmother followed her gaze. "How different things would be if he had lived. You'd still be welcome at home, even."

"Yes, probably," Kitty agreed. "But it is part of the Lord's will we don't understand. His ideas about running the world don't always agree with ours." She hoped the old woman would not take her statement as sass.

The grandmother's eyes radiated disapproval. "You speak so personally of the Holy Father."

Kitty nodded. "The Son is a personal Savior to me. God is no longer the frightening or terrible creature he appeared to be in my childhood."

Her grandmother shivered, picked up her crocheting and changed the subject. "Your mother and her husband stopped here last week."

"I was hoping she would be able to do so. She brought me some dishtowels she had made for me."

"And are you back in good graces with your stepfather?"

Kitty shook her head.

"I suppose deep down he is a good man. If your mother would just have followed my orders when my son died, things would be much better for you."

It was not the time to reveal anger, but Kitty recalled again what this woman and her daughters had tried to force on her mother. She held her words, controlled her temper and refused to give her grandmother the adventure of an answer.

"Unfortunately, your mother is just as stubborn as I am. She lived alone on the farm my son had provided until she could no longer stand to raise four little girls by herself. But I'm sure the man married her for the farm." The old woman's hand shook as she poured coffee into dainty china cups and set them on the new, but dull, yellow oilcloth covering the round table. "He's a hard worker, he is, but he sure could be a bit more godly."

"Perhaps he has a godliness we don't understand," Kitty offered meekly, surprised she would even attempt to justify Pop's behavior.

The grandmother shook her head. "You're the one I don't understand. But no matter. Sit yourself down and have coffee with me."

Kitty stifled a shrug as well as an answer. Instead she sat down at the kitchen table.

Because the elderly lady belonged to a class of people who believe all guests arrive at their kitchens half-starved, she opened a tin of sliced peaches, spooned them into a cut glass bowl and set it near the bread slices. "Eat up, girl. You are much too skinny to be getting married." She added milk and sugar for the coffee on a shiny, tiny tin platter.

The grandmother set herself daintily on the chair across the table from Kitty. She buttered a slice of bread and nibbled at it a bit before speaking again. "I've met your young man. He's very handsome. Probably not very intelligent, but good looking regardless."

Kitty was thankful she had cooled the coffee with cream as she was just taking a sip when the old lady made her observation. She choked, shot coffee through her nose and teared up, all in one horrible moment.

The grandmother handed her a cloth napkin and went prattling on. "He does come from a good family, and if he's half the man his brother is, you will never be hungry." She worked on her bread a bit more, then, "I see you are already wearing a ring. You get your ring ahead of the wedding?"

"It's an engagement ring, Grandma."

"What a waste of hard-earned money. But I suppose you can get some money out of it when your baby has pneumonia and needs a doctor or when your man dies like your father did."

Kitty finished her snack as quickly as possible and got up to leave, but before she walked out the door, her grandmother calmly led her into the bedroom where she opened a large trunk. From it she took two handmade rag rugs done up in beautiful color combinations and laid them in Kitty's arms.

On top of them she laid a wedding ring design quilt. "Here's a few things to brighten your new home."

The girl bent to kiss the weathered old cheek, mopped tears from her own, and fled.

CHAPTER THIRTEEN

"When it's nighttime in Nevada, I'm dreaming
Of the old days, on the prairie, with you."

It was Saturday night and he was singing with his guitar. Twyla had turned the lamp down low before she joined Frank and the baby in their bedroom. Kitty was curled up in the rocking chair, watching her beloved as he sang. She reflected on the evening they had just spent.

"Nice coat," he had said as he held it for her to slip into before leaving the hotel. "Is this the one your mom brought you?"

"Yes." She stood there for a bit, thinking.

"Okay, let's hear it. I see something running around that pretty face of yours. Something connected to your brain."

"Let's head for the theatre and I'll tell you." When they were out on the sidewalk, she went on. "It's a memory, probably one of the earliest I have. Mom had just made me a coat, a very special coat, but I cannot remember the color, or maybe it was a coat of many colors. Anyway, our house caught on fire in the early morning. We all got out safely, but I tried to go back for my new coat. It was hanging right inside the door. They wouldn't let me go."

He tenderly wiped her tears with the pads of his thumbs. "I'm sorry. But I'm glad they protected you."

They had gone on to the movie, "They Gave Him A Gun," starring Spencer Tracy. It was an anti-war story featuring a man gone wild on the battlefield and then back home became a gangster. Kitty hated the show, but she didn't know how Brice felt about it, so they had traveled out to Frank and Twyla's place without saying much of anything.

Kitty made a batch of fudge and Frank made popcorn and they had played a few hands of cards and enjoyed the snacks before the others went to bed.

Now, after an hour of some kissing, some singing and some conversation or just quietly thinking, they would drift off to bed.

She made herself comfortable on the couch and he went to the extra bedroom.

Sometimes on Sunday morning they drove to the little Lutheran Church not far from his parents' home. Sometimes, they ate a late breakfast with Frank and Twyla.

It was a weekend routine Kitty would love to repeat up until the day they married and moved to their own house.

Another week, when Brice had not shown up for Friday night's movie, she assumed he was picking corn on his job. Knowing that every dollar might eventually buy groceries, she did not mind. In the same fashion, even though she caught a cold and spent a day in bed, she made sure she got up and went to her job at the theatre. Her fifty-cent wage could buy ten pounds of sugar.

Saturday night Frank was waiting for her when she came out of the theatre. As he drove her out into the country toward his home, he explained. "Brice has been sick."

"Oh no, he caught my cold."

"Not exactly," Frank hesitated. "Has he told you about his spells?"

"Spells?"

"Apparently not." He drove on in silence.

"What do you mean, spells?"

"You can ask him in the morning?"

"In the morning?" Kitty felt really dumb.

"He's in Van Metre, playing for a dance. Do you want to go?"

"Is Twyla going?"

"No. But she said you should go and I should dance with you. And your friend Eve will be there."

"My friend Eve?" She felt dumber. "I thought she was Brice's old girlfriend."

"They practically grew up together. I don't think you have anything to worry about there."

"Brice gets jealous really quick-like. Do you think he minds me dancing with you?"

"Nope. He trusts us. Just like Twyla trusts us."

"I s'pose I'll go, then."

The dance was in full swing when they arrived. Kitty waved at her brown-eyed guitar picker and received a smile and nod in return.

After a round or two of square dancing, Brice's sister Angel led off on a sad, solemn tune and a plaintive sound turned heads to see Kitty's beloved playing a new instrument.

"A violin." She breathed to Frank. "I didn't know he played a violin, too."

"It's a fiddle."

"What's the difference?"

"The guy who's playing it. And probably the kind of music played on it."

"Well, whatever it is, I like it."

The violin was still leading the band with "Beautiful Dreamer" when Eve slipped up and whispered to Kitty. "I need to find the outhouse. Will you come with me?"

"Sure." Kitty slipped into her coat.

The two young ladies made their way past the crowd of young men who loitered near the dance hall door.

Outside, a full moon lit the way past the cars and down the road.

"I sure hope you know where we are going."

"Oh yeah. I've been here lots of times during the day and even on darker nights. We cross this little wooden bridge and go over behind the Callihan house. They have a nice privy. It doesn't even smell."

"How could it in this cold weather? I'll bet it smells just as bad as anyone else's in the summer time."

"Ah, who cares?" After they crossed the bridge, Eve led the way along a yard fence, through a gate and down a path to the little building.

On their way back to the dance hall, Eve leaned up against the wooden bridge railing. "Wow, look at that moon."

"Yup. Pretty one."

"So. You gonna marry my old pal, Brice?"

"Yes. Do you mind?"

"Maybe. Maybe not."

"Did he kiss you?"

Eve whipped around to grab the lapels of Kitty's coat. "Does it make any difference to you? You got him now." She started off on an angry stomp. Kitty trailed behind as they approached the dance hall.

A fist fight had begun just outside the door. Most of the young men who had been standing around inside had moved outside to watch and cheer on the fighters.

Eve pushed her way through the group with Kitty tagging close behind. Just as they reached the door, a sort-of-familiar cowboy stepped up and circled Kitty into his arms. "Hey, hey. I know you."

"Well, I don't know you," she struggled.

"Calm down, little heifer. Remember the day the H Bar H was moving cattle on the road that leads to your sistah's house? You smiled so pretty at me. Hey, you and me could have us a good time."

Kitty nearly panicked when she realized Eve had left her to go on into the dance hall. She tried stomping the man's foot, but he was too quick.

"Hey, just a little peck, huh?" He was tugging her away from the hall. "Let's slip around the corner, and…"

"Let go of my brother's woman."

He let go and got in Frank's face. "You wanna fight your brother's fight, then?"

"I do not fight with fists," Frank replied, ducking the punch aimed in his direction, catching the arm, flipping the body directly into the crowd of spectators. "Get in the hall, Kitty."

She hurried along the edge of the dancers to an empty bench near the stage. She managed to keep from crying, but felt the evening had been spoiled.

Moments later Brice left the stage and came to dance with her. Silently he guided her around the dance floor, thankful he and his brother had been the ones to teach her the steps. Her timing was perfect. But then she leaked tears on the front of his white shirt. When she could talk, she told him she had loved the violin music.

"Fiddle." He teased. "It will be coming with me to our home. Dad told me long ago it would be mine as soon as I had a home of my own. His father bought the fiddle off a peddler or traded something for it. It has been around as long as I can remember."

After their song finished, he led her closer to the stage. Frank whispered a few words to his brother, who nodded, then they both spoke to their sister.

"Last dance," the vocalist announced, and the band swung into "Be it ever so humble, there's no place like home."

He drove her back to the hotel Sunday evening. She finally got up her nerve to question him.

"Frank said you had a spell on Saturday. What did he mean?"

He didn't answer immediately and she hoped he wasn't angry.

"The doctor calls it epilepsy. Mom says it isn't, but that the doctor calls it that so I can avoid the draft."

"Isn't that what the kid in the Bible had when he threw himself into the fire or into the river?"

"He had a demon, or maybe several of them. This is not a demon."

"How do you know it's not?"

"Because Jesus is Lord, near me, inside of me. There's no room for a demon."

"Oh. That's good. So, you don't throw yourself in the river?"

"In the summertime, sometimes," he smiled. "But only to cool off and enjoy a good swim." He patted her knee.

"Actually, I have no warning when a spell is going to happen until it actually starts happening. Almost always, it starts when I wake up in the morning. Do you know what aura means?"

"Like aura borealis?"

"Not exactly. I think you mean northern lights, and that is Aurora Borealis. But some of the effects are the same. I might roll over in bed when I first wake up and it will feel like the room is slowing moving in a circle. Sometimes the motion makes me sick to my stomach. And even with my eyes closed, I can see wavy lines at the outside corners of my eyes."

She was stunned.

He continued, "the scary part is when I cannot talk. That doesn't happen very often, but when it does, it makes me feel…a little bit crazy."

"I'm sorry, hon."

"I know I should have told you about it a long time ago. But I always hope each spell is going to be the last one and I had not had one for months until yesterday morning."

The pain she felt for him only worsened with his next words.

"If you want out of the picture, you can still do so."

She looked quickly at his face and felt his tan was looking a little gray. "I think you need me. I'm not backing out on our deal. Not ever. Nope. No matter what happens."

"Thanks," he whispered.

It was enough.

♪♪♪

Christmas 1937 fell on a Sunday, making a long weekend for Kitty. Her employer sent her off with a new pair of mittens and a wish for a good holiday.

She and Brice, Frank and Twyla and the baby went to Angel and Pete's house on Christmas Eve where they had supper, made candy, played cards, hung up stockings and entertained the children until it was time for them to be in bed.

Christmas morning they traveled to the little Immanuel Lutheran Church south of Van Metre. Frank and Brice sang during the Christmas program. Kitty had heard that they made a great duet, but had not before heard them other than singing little ditties with the guitar.

When the church service was over, Frank, Twyla and baby drove over the hills and east to have dinner with Mom, Pop and the "kids." Brice and Kitty had their own beef roast and spuds in Twyla's kitchen.

Then they walked to the dam east of the house and went ice skating.

He had her back to the hotel before 7:30, as was the rule, whether they liked it or not. March fifth could not come soon enough.

In spite of lonely times when he was off working somewhere, the days of January and February blended together to rush by.

She wrote in her diary that on a "beautiful night" she saw a "beautiful movie" and wished he could be there with her. "God's Country and the Woman" was in Technicolor and she loved the story even though she could not have named the actors the next day.

She learned to tat, and read, and worked hard at the hotel. She sold tickets at the theatre and watched the popular movies that came to town. She missed him tremendously when they were not together and clung to every moment when they were.

He took her out to Frank's to see the heifer with her brand new calf and knew there would be milk for their table.

She worked one last day at the hotel and woke up on March 5, 1938, her nineteenth birthday.

♪ ♪ ♪

They were married on a day of such brilliant sunshine the snow glittered, making them squint when they were outdoors and pause upon going inside to let their eyes adjust to the dim light.

Her mail-order catalog dress was of royal blue jersey with long lacy sleeves. She wore no hat on her brown, curly hair.

Besides the preacher, Frank and Twyla were the only ones present. They heard his brother and her sister say their vows and saw Brice put the little wire band next to the basket weave diamond chip ring on Kitty's finger. Then they added their signatures to the piece of parchment which tied the couple together until death would part them.

After the simple ceremony in the parsonage of the Methodist Church, all four young people drove to the hotel to collect Kitty's belongings. Then they stopped at the grocery store to buy a box of staple foods, such as a slab of bacon, oatmeal, salt, brown sugar, baking powder, baking soda and a small bottle of vanilla.

Kitty noted a pretty blue-flowered sack of flour and whispered to Brice, "What about flour?"

He shook his head, but as soon as they were out of the store, he explained. "A sack costs seven dollars. I ordered a half-barrel of flour from Sears and Roebuck. We can use the barrel for a chair when we need an extra."

"What did the barrel cost?"

"Three dollars and forty-seven cents. Still more than we can afford, but something we have to have, I'd think. Can't make pancakes without it."

Frank and Twyla drove them to their place on the creek.

"Leave us out here at the gate," Brice requested. "We will walk up to the house."

He carried the box of groceries and she toted her bundle as they walked silently up the lane on the small farm, which would be their first home together.

Kitty saw the team of horses and the milking heifer in the corral by the barn. She knew the new calf was locked in the barn away from his mother so she would have milk for their table. On other days the calf would be locked up at night, so they could have morning milk. She saw smoke rising from the chimney and knew he had started a fire in the cook stove before coming to get her. She hoped the warmth would chase the chill of fear from her innermost being.

The snow on the porch roof was melting in the afternoon sun so water dripped from the eaves. She heard a trickle as it ran off the roof of the house and into a rain barrel at the corner.

They left their overshoes on the porch and walked into the kitchen. Brice stirred the coals in the range and laid wood on them. She followed him as he carried wood into the other room and stirred the fire in the heater they had talked of buying the first time she saw the house.

"I didn't take the chairs out of the crates. I thought you would like to help me."

"By all means." Kitty hung her coat on one of the hooks by the door. "Didn't you say my wedding band was inside one of the boxes the chairs came in?"

“No, it was taped to the top of one of them. Sears, Roebuck and Company must have thought it would take such a heavy band to keep us together they had to send it by freight.”

“I’m just glad it didn’t get lost,” Kitty twisted the band around her finger and admired the shining, white gold. “I think it goes nicely with the engagement ring.” She moved across the room to help him. “Did they send bedding by freight train too?”

“No, it came several days later to the post office. I’m glad your employer gave you those old blankets. This one we ordered might not have kept us warm in a blizzard.”

“I thought it was nice of her to give us a collection of jelly glasses, too. I hadn’t thought about what we were going to use to drink our milk.”

“I have three soup bowls from boxes of oatmeal and a couple old plates Mom had stuck away in her pantry,” he added. “One of them must be warped or something because it spins when you try to eat from it.”

“We'll call it Old Spinny,” she giggled.

When the four wooden chairs were taken from the crates and admired, they took two to the kitchen and set them by the round wooden table. The other two they left in the living room.

Kitty gathered the bedding in her arms. “I’ll run upstairs and make up the bed.”

“Then I’ll go out and milk the cow and feed a bit of hay. Put on your coat. It’s chilly upstairs. Don’t fuss over supper. Your sister sent over some cold roast beef and a loaf of bread, some butter, too, I think.”

“God bless Twyla.”

He took the shiny new pail from its place in the pantry. Then the kitchen door closed behind him and Kitty went upstairs.

In the bedroom she noticed the mattress and fat pillows he had brought from his parents’ home. Then she saw the old sewing machine cabinet she had noted on their first visit to the house. New boards had been neatly fitted across the entire top to form a dressing table. Those boards had been sanded, stained and polished until the finish was soft as a baby’s cheek. On the wall above it glittered a new mirror with an attached note:

“Happy Birthday to the prettiest nineteen year old I know.”

Tears stung her eyelids. “And I thought he was not sentimental.” She trailed her fingers across the top of the dressing table.

Then she turned to the bed. Taking the new muslin sheets from their wrappers, she spread them over the mattress, smoothed out the wrinkles and tucked under the edges as her hotel manager had taught her. She added the blankets from the hotel and at last spread the colorful topper from Sears and Roebuck. In the morning she would add the wedding ring quilt from her grandmother, but of course it would not be for everyday use unless they needed it for warmth.

When she had covered the pillows with the fancy cases Ginger had embroidered and fluffed them into place, she stood back to approve the job. She became aware of her hands shaking and it wasn’t from the cold. She felt nervous as she went to the window and stared down at the dirty brown floor of the yard and wished for a moment she could flee across the pasture to her sister’s refuge.

She saw him coming from the barn with the milk pail in one hand and a smaller container in the other, which she assumed was the day’s contribution from the few hens he had brought from his mother’s flock. He walked tall and confidently and even from the distance she could feel the warmth in his brown eyes and she knew he was singing some song. In a flash of understanding, her fear turned to excitement. Loving this man until the day she died was going to be one grand journey.

She hurried downstairs to set out their supper. When he brought in the milk she strained it through an old dishtowel, poured two jelly jars full, and set the rest in a big jar on a shelf in the pantry to cool. She noticed he had turned the sagging boards, which were already beginning to straighten.

“It won’t be long until we have to take stuff to the cellar to keep it cool. Spring is coming.”

“And I’m glad, even though it hasn’t been a hard winter.”

When they had eaten, she lit the kerosene lamp before clearing away the things from the table.

And then he pulled her on to his lap and hugged her tight. She melted into the warmth of his broad chest, listened to the strong thump of his heart, inhaled the scent of his soap. She closed her eyes as he kissed the top of her head.

Her voice was soft. "Once you sang about a little green valley. Won't you play your guitar and sing it again for me tonight?"

"Why that one?"

"Because a little green valley with cattle and horses grazing is part of our dream." She left his lap to finish clearing the table.

When she had finished, she joined him near the heater in the living room, sat near him in one of their new chairs and in the gathering dusk, he sang just for her.

"I hear a Mockingbird, down in the little green valley
He's singing out his heart to welcome me.
There she waits by the garden gate, down in the little green valley.
When I get home again how happy she will be."

The snow came without a sound in the night. In the morning Kitty slipped out from under the covers, shivered into her clothes and hurried downstairs to start a fire in each stove.

She shook down the ashes in the cook stove until the grate was clear. Then she crumpled pages from an old newspaper and put them on the grate. She added kindling on top of the paper and lit the paper with flame from a match she struck on the side of the matchbox. When the fire was roaring and snapping, she added several bigger pieces of wood. She set the tin wash basin of water on the stove to warm. Then she took water from the stove's well, put it in a saucepan and set it to boil for oatmeal. From there she went to the living room, built a fire in the stove in there, and then returned to the kitchen to make the cereal.

Brice came downstairs, kissed her for a long moment before he sat down to put on the high-laced shoes he carried in his hand and then reminded her to add a little salt to the oatmeal.

By the time the cereal was cooked, the fire had died down to bright coals. Kitty moved one of the round lids away from its slot and used a long-handled fork to toast slices of bread over the coals. Brice buttered the slices and placed them on one of the two new plates, which had been a gift from Frank and Twyla. With jam for their toast and milk, cream and brown sugar for the oatmeal, they shared their first breakfast as man and wife.

When they had finished, Brice put on his cap and coat and went outside to do morning chores. Frank drove in before he had finished.

While he waited for Brice, Frank stood on the rag rug just inside the door and chatted with Kitty while she tidied the kitchen.

"How's Twyla and the baby?"

"Fine," he answered. "Do you have enough reading material to keep you busy during the long days while Brice is gone working?"

"I think so. All those books and magazines you brought here to the house should last a long time. I also splurged and bought a crochet hook and some thread. I'll see what I can do with my three thumbs."

He nodded. "Do you know how to use a sewing machine?"

"No," she looked doubtful, "but I'm a quick learner."

"Good. I'm sure Twyla will be glad to teach you on her machine. I think she told you to bring your laundry over to our house, too, and use our washing machine until you get one of your own."

"Yes, she did tell me. I am so thankful you kids live so close to us kids."

When Brice came in with the milk, he handed the pail to her, gave her his warmest smile and the brothers left for the day.

It was suddenly very lonely in the big, quiet house. Her comfort was in believing sundown would bring him back to her arms.

So they settled into the routine of daily living until one night when the large moon set the snow aglitter and lit up the outside world.

He was late coming home, so she took the kerosene lantern to the barn and milked the cow. The moon gave so much light, she refused to light the lantern until she stepped into the darkness of the big barn. Then she struck a match and set a glow in the lantern to make a dim yellow light that cast long shadows on the barn walls.

The cow came in from the barnyard when Kitty opened the door. And while the animal was eating oats from her feed box, the girl took care of the milking chore.

She was back in the kitchen straining the milk when Brice drove into the yard. She set the cast iron skillet over the heat to fry potatoes and eggs for his supper.

He stomped on the porch to knock excess snow from his boots, and then his presence filled the little kitchen and wrapped its arms around Kitty.

"Beautiful night," he murmured against her hair, "just right for a chivaree."

She stiffened. "A what?"

"Chivaree, where all the neighbors come in to greet the newlyweds."

"And isn't it also where they run off with the bride or make her bake a cake for them to eat?"

"And tip over the privy and put corncobs in the bed, hide the crank for the car, sew your nightgown together across the bottom."

She backed up from him far enough to focus the biggest glare she could come up with. "And it is obvious you have previously been active in such events."

"Oh, a couple, maybe." He hung his coat on the back of the chair and sat down to unlace his boots. "Do you think our love can endure it all?"

"Yes," she was serious, "but I'm not sure my temper can. I like things just the way they are. Why would anyone want to mess up our house?"

"Oh, this neighborhood is a pretty decent crowd. We won't get it as rough as some newlyweds do."

He slid his chair up to the table to eat supper. "And if we get the chance, we'll have a little fun of our own. First of all, we'll make them look for us. With all the snow, I don't think they will try sneaking in any way but on the road. And this bright moonlight doesn't give much cover. We can see them coming and slip out of the house when the first car turns into our lane."

"What if they make me bake a cake? You know I have trouble enough baking something without anyone standing around watching. I know I'll burn it. I always do."

"Bake a pancake for them. You make the best pancakes in the country."

"Only because Mrs. Severson taught me the basics and you gave me tips to make them the best." She sat down near him. "Do you really think they will carry me away?"

He shrugged. "Don't worry about it. I'm not even sure they're coming tonight. I just had a hunch they might."

Her shaking hands revealed how nervous she was as she washed and dried their dishes and wiped the table. He blew out the flame in the lamp on the table and they moved into the living room.

Brice played his guitar and sang to Kitty where she sat near the window, staring out into the moonlit darkness.

Suddenly she laughed. "Suppose we sit watching like this every night until summer and no one comes. This could get old in a hurry."

"Oh, I don't know. I imagine playing and singing for you while you sit so prettily in the moonlight could never get old for me."

"Thank you," she whispered, then stiffened. "Come here." He could hear the tremor in her voice.

When he looked out the window he saw big, dark shadows of several cars moving slowly along the road with their lights turned off.

"Now we can't get out of the house without them seeing us. Let's hide." He led her to the pantry, stopping to pick up the unlit lamp from the table, which he set on a shelf. He closed the door leading into the kitchen. "We don't want to have the lamp knocked off the table and broken when they stumble around in the darkness trying to find us." He sat down on the flour barrel and cuddled her on his lap.

Kitty shivered in excitement, her breath coming short as she wondered if he could hear her heart pounding. "What if they think we are gone? Will they leave?"

"Not until they've turned the place upside down looking for us," he whispered in return. "And with the car in the yard they aren't very apt to think we've left the place. I can't hear any motors running, so they must be walking in from the road."

"I wish they'd hurry. I can't stand suspense, not even in a Zane Grey book." Kitty's legs were shaking. "Won't we feel foolish when they find us in the pantry?"

"Probably, but it's all part of the fun." He shushed her with a long kiss.

They heard the porch floor creak, and then creak again. Then such a racket burst forth Kitty lurched before hiding her face against Brice's shoulder. People were shouting and banging pan lids and blowing whistles. Someone set off a string of firecrackers.

The kitchen door scraped open and silence reigned momentarily. "They've gone to bed already," someone shouted and the sound was like a herd of cattle tromping up the stairs to the second floor.

A baby cried near the pantry, and then the door swung open and the couple was revealed in lantern light.

Twyla's laugh rang out, "The queen was in the pantry, eating bread and honey…"

"Yes?" added a voice, "but what's the hired man doing in there with her?" The lantern light revealed a tall, muscular woman swinging a huge coffee pot up on the cook stove. "Stir up the fire, Brice. This coffee is starting to cool already."

"I hope you brought cups or cans. We have a grand total of two, three if you count my shaving mug," Brice grumbled in reply.

"Oh yes. We took care of everything."

Frank hollered up the stairs, "Hey, they're in the kitchen."

Soon the light of several lanterns lit up the house. People crowded into the living room and sat on the floor or stood around talking. Two young men carried coats upstairs, but before piling them on the bed, they turned back the covers and emptied their pockets of corncobs. After they had turned up the bottom of the top sheet and tucked it in securely to short sheet the bed, they neatly remade it before arranging a safe nest of coats for Twyla's Spoofy.

The sparse furniture in the two downstairs rooms was shoved up against the wall, then Brice's sister took her push and pull accordion from its box, someone handed Brice his guitar and a fiddle appeared. After a quick tuning, the music began.

Kitty was standing near Brice, her foot tapping to the rollicking sweet song when Twyla came to her from the kitchen. "We forgot to bring sugar for the coffee and I can't find any in your pantry. Will you come find it for me?"

"I can find some brown sugar for you," Kitty followed her sister toward the kitchen. The moment she stepped through the doorway, a blanket was thrown over her head and strong arms carried her from the house through the kitchen entry.

Laughter and shouts came to her dimly through the smothering darkness of the blanket. Her captor struggled across uneven ground with his burden.

"Get to the barn with her. She'll freeze out here without a coat." Frank's voice.

"Ah, it ain't so awful cold out. And I don't know the barn. I'll run into something in the dark."

"Nothing more than a cow pie. Anyway, I know the barn pretty well. Hurry up. They won't be able to hold him in there very long."

"He's making music. He won't miss her."

"You've been married too long," Frank laughed.

When they stepped inside the barn, her captor put his burden down to stand on her trembling legs.

"Let's get the blanket off her. She can't climb the ladder to the hay loft with it wrapped around her."

"All right, but make sure it goes in the loft with her," Frank ordered. "We don't need her catching cold." After a moment, he added, "How are you going to keep her from screaming? The blanket might muffle the sound a bit."

"She hasn't screamed yet. Maybe she ain't the screaming kind." He pulled off the blanket, "You try screaming and I'll kiss you."

The scream died in her throat as Frank's voice warned. "You kiss her and after Brice half kills you, I'll finish the job."

The other man swore, "I was only kidding."

"She's an innocent young woman. She doesn't believe you were kidding." Frank found the ladder to the loft and whispered. "Up the ladder, girlie girl, then you can have your blanket back."

In the loft, Frank carried her to a pile of hay and pushed her up on top of it. As she lay face down, trembling from the cold and something close to rage, Frank spread the blanket over her.

"How many feeding holes are there in this loft floor?" Her other abductor queried.

"Four, maybe five," Frank replied, "all covered the last time I was in here, which was years ago. There are little slots around the edges to push hay through, but not big enough to allow a person to escape."

"Do you think he will look here for her?"

"Sooner or later. Bones knew where we were taking her. I told him he could tip off Brice after a bit of anxiety."

"He won't need tipping off," Kitty thought. "These characters left the top barn door open. We always shut it at night."

"I'm going somewhere where I can see the house. Sounds to me like they let him out." Frank stated.

"How am I supposed to guard all four holes? He will be able to find any one of them in the dark and get the cover moved over."

"Ah, they won't let him up here," Frank's voice faded into the darkness.

Kitty was sad to hear the closing of both upper and lower barn doors, thereby covering her only clue for Brice. She was even more worried at the idea of Frank leaving her alone with the man who threatened kisses.

After a few minutes of chilled silence, her captor whispered, "Don't run off, gal. I'm going to find an escape route in case he does get up here." He rustled off the stack and into the darkness.

Kitty knew she had no chance of reaching one of the big holes in the loft floor. She also knew the hay slides were too small for a man to get through. But she wasn't a man.

Without a sound, she pushed herself backward over the hay, leaving the blanket in a bunch as a decoy. The hay let her slide down without noise, muffling her feet when they struck the loft floor behind the haystack.

She crawled the short distance to the wall, feeling her way ahead with her hands until she located an opening in the floor of the haymow, then she slipped down through it, hung for a moment by her hands and then dropped to the ground. Disoriented in the darkness, she had no idea where the north door might be, but moved along the wall, placing one foot in front of the other to avoid tripping over frozen cow pies. A noisy rustle overhead was an unwelcome danger.

"Hey! Frank! She's gone! Frank!"

Kitty plunged for the crack of light from outside, threw back the latch and leaped outside, directly into the arms of a man she didn't know.

But without the blanket smothering her, she was not to be held. She lashed out with arms and legs in such ferocity, her captor lost hold. She slipped in the snow, jumped up, ran, stumbled, but then ran again.

Running feet sounded close behind her while her goal of the porch seemed a faraway place. There was no place to hide. For a moment she considered the privy, but what if they locked her in there? She was already chilled.

A shout rang out behind her, "Hold him, you guys."

Then she saw the man on the porch, blocking her entry into the house. A helpless cry choked in her throat. She knew somewhere behind her there were strong arms holding Brice and before her a huge bear of a man was in her way. She plunged on, thinking, "I'll clobber somebody if I have to."

Just as her trembling legs gained the porch, familiar arms swept her up. "I've got you, darling."

"He wins!" Frank shouted from somewhere behind them.

"Let us in," Brice ordered. "This gal is half-frozen." He carried her into the house.

The tall woman who had put the coffee pot on to boil poured a cup of the steaming liquid and put it in Kitty's hands after she had laced it with sugar and cream.

The girl caught her trembling bottom lip with her teeth as she fought back tears. Brice squeezed her shoulder. "It's okay, honey. It's all over now. You'll be queen for the rest of the night."

The tall woman smiled. "You have a lot of spunk for a little gal. You'll make it all right in this neighborhood."

The men, who had been outside, tramped into the kitchen. Her captor walked over to Kitty and gave her an exasperating hug. “How did you get out of the loft without me seeing you?”

Frank answered for her, even as he ruffled Twyla’s curls with one big hand. “These girls Brice and I caught are little enough to crawl out of a mouse hole.”

“Well, as fast as she can run, I’m surprised you caught them at all.”

Kitty laughed. The genuine warmth of the people was thawing her reserve.

She was amazed at the quantity of food the neighbors had brought. There were stacks of sandwiches, plates of cookies and wide slices of cake.

“I always thought the new bride had to provide the food at chivarees,” Kitty attempted weakly.

“Not in this neighborhood,” the tall woman tending the coffee replied. “Nobody here had anything when we first started off. And most of us lost what we did have during the Dirty Thirties, but those of us who stayed here on the land are sure ‘nuf going to share with you all.”

“And if there is food left when we are finished tonight, it stays here for you young folks. Also, do not hope to return any plates or cups left behind. They are for you to keep. Now, pile some food on a napkin and take yourselves into the other room. Seeing you will bring the others after their lunch.”

Brice and Kitty followed her request, seating themselves on the floor in the living room.

When everyone had finished eating, they began to pull on coats, caps and scarves. And then with warm wishes for the new couple, they drifted away into the night.

After all the other folks had left, Frank and Twyla and Spoofy lingered in the kitchen.

“We are driving over to Mom’s on Sunday,” Twyla remarked as she spread the baby’s blankets out on the table for wrapping. “Why don’t you come with us?”

“You could pick up the young hens your mom promised,” added Frank.

Brice and Kitty exchanged a glance, then he spoke, "It's okay with me if Kitty wants to go."

"Haven't you been home yet?" Frank inquired.

Kitty shook her head slowly. "Not since the summer day I walked into a new way of living. Seems like a long time ago. I'm not sure I have the nerve to go home yet."

Twyla frolicked into song. "And now we are married, we are, Mama. And now we are married, we are, ha ha. And now we are married, we are, Mama. And you can tell Pa 'cause he can't help it at all."

"What did he do when you came home married?"

"You were there. Don't you remember?"

"He treated her like a queen," Frank inserted.

"You are the one, sister. He was always kinder to you than the rest of us, but probably because you tried the hardest to get along with him."

"Maybe. But he does have a heart under his turtle shell."

"If only he would let Jesus soften his shell," Kitty mused. "If only he knew a little of Mom's faith."

"Are you sure he doesn't?"

"Well, if he does have any faith, it sure doesn't show. Seems to me it ought to show."

"Suppose," Frank suggested, "you wait until after Sunday to make a judgment. If he forgives you for running away, then he has one Christ-like virtue, doesn't he?

Kitty nodded. And then Twyla asked, "Have you forgiven him?"

"I think so," Kitty was quick to answer. "I don't understand him. Maybe I never will. But I think I've forgiven him. In his own way he did a lot for us girls."

"Right." Twyla centered the baby on the blankets and wrapped her snugly. "We better go home and let these people get to bed. There isn't much sleeping time left before dawn."

Frank snickered and his eyes met Twyla's mischievous face.

Brice jumped up and reached for his coat. "I believe we'll go sleep at your house. You folks can have our bed for tonight. Then you won't have to take Spoofy out in the cold."

"Oh no, you don't. We had to sleep in our own chivaree bed."

"Yes, but Kitty didn't get to help mess up your bed."

"Oh? How unfortunate. And I notice you did not include yourself in your statement." Frank was laughing as he opened the door for Twyla. "Turnabout is fair play and besides, we didn't get to help mess up your bed either."

Then they were gone and Brice hugged Kitty close. "Happy?"

"Yes, and accepted, even if we have to clean up a mess before we sleep tonight."

"Maybe it will only be corncobs in our bed. Then we can at least use them for fuel for the cook stove."

"Let's go see how bad it really is."

CHAPTER FOURTEEN

The road to her mother's house on Sunday morning made a twisted path across Kitty's heart. On her lap she balanced a tall cake of Twyla's creation, using care not to smear the snowy frosting. Her own contribution to the dinner, a cast iron skillet full of escalloped potatoes and bacon, stayed warm in a cardboard box on the floor of Frank's car.

The trip seemed to last forever, until she saw familiar fences and pastures flashing by the windows of the car. The old schoolhouse sat lonely in the corner of a pasture. Long grass and weeds trapped snow in the yard and the peeling paint made the building look forlorn.

"How many times did you get bucked off in the schoolyard?" Twyla's voice trespassed on Kitty's thoughts.

"Never often enough to learn to fall gracefully," Kitty laughed. "But at least once a day when Bronco was a colt."

"And you were a wild young filly," Brice whispered.

Kitty jabbed his side with her elbow. "I dented up more syrup pail lunch buckets than anyone else."

"Good thing you didn't have a fancy flowered store-bought box like cousin Dell," Twyla remarked.

"I'll bet cousin Dell never carried cold bean sandwiches either."

"No, she always made fancy things like horses doovers," Twyla laughed.

"Horses' whats?" Frank exclaimed.

"Well, I suppose it is a French word. Anyway, the spelling is h-o-r-s d'-o-e-u-v-r-e-s."

"Doesn't sound very good, but I suppose if you ever cook in French, I'll eat it."

"Don't invite me over." Brice interjected. "I prefer beef to horse meat."

"How would you know? You wouldn't have the heart to eat horse meat."

"I'll bet he could if he got hungry enough."

The car roared up a long hill. Having spotted the approaching car, Mom was out on the porch, waiting to hug them all and carry the baby into the house.

In the kitchen she drew away the outer blankets and smiled down at the squirming infant. Kitty tingled to see the love in her mother's eyes.

Then Grace and Ginger came in from the chill of outdoors. Frank and Brice escaped to the cheery solitude of the living room and left the ladies in the kitchen chattering like busy hens in a dust bath.

"I must have known you were coming," Mom said, giving the baby over to Ginger. "I have a big roast in the oven. We butchered about two weeks ago, so we've been enjoying lots of good beef."

With gentle hands Kitty pushed her mother on to a chair. "You relax. I brought potatoes and Twyla baked a cake for dessert. Now, you tell me what kind of vegetables you want for dinner and I'll run down to the cellar for a jar or two."

"Oh, corn, of course. Your favorite. And bring up some pickles." Mom caught her youngest daughter's hands in her own work-reddened, strong members. Their eyes met as Mom whispered. "Kitty, is everything all right?"

"I couldn't be happier, Mom. He is such a wonderful, gentle man."

"You're so pale and skinny."

Her answer was almost inaudible. "And I'm scared spitless about seeing Pop again."

Mom smiled in relief. “Oh, don't worry about him. He's like a mellowed old bear. Bring up some apples, too. We will make a quick sauce to go with the cake.”

Kitty lifted the cellar door in the porch floor and slipped the holding strap over its hook, which kept the strap in place. She bounced down the stairs, pausing at the bottom to strike a match and light the small lantern hanging from the floor joists overhead. In the cool dimness of the cellar she sucked in the aroma of winter apples and big onions. Her eyes noted the pile of potatoes in their bin, far from the apples and onions because any good gardener knew one did not store apples and potatoes together. She marveled once more at the multitude of jars in colorful rows on the shelves. She chose two jars of corn and a jar of dill pickles. “Brice loves watermelon pickles,” she remembered and added a jar of those to her selection before returning upstairs.

Ginger, who was rocking the baby in her arms, called to Kitty, “I suppose you'll be bringing one of these around pretty soon, huh?

“Good night. Give me time.”

“Well, what other reason would you get married for? Or did you just want to get out of having to work?”

“You haven't mellowed any since you got way from my influence,” Kitty replied, reaching for silverware to help set the table. “I thought since you didn't have me around to pick on, you might find more productive ways to use your voice.”

“And I can see marriage has not improved your disposition much. I figured you might use up all your nastiness on your old man, then you could be nice to me.”

“No chance,” Kitty returned in good humor. “I wouldn't miss your snotty remarks for anything. If you'd get a man for yourself, maybe you'd be nicer.”

“Oh no. You're not getting me into your trap. Just because you and Twyla acted like fools.” Ginger was pacing with the baby, coaxing her to stop fussing. She paused near Kitty and lowered her voice, “besides, you took the man I really wanted.”

“Enough,” Mom snapped in an unusual tone. “Do you girls have to quarrel?”

"Oh, we aren't quarreling," Kitty replied and paused from her work to hug both baby and sister. "We're just renewing old times."

"Well, it isn't any prettier now than it used to be. You both need to grow up and let a little love shine through, if for no other reason than the little one you're holding in your arms. She doesn't need to grow up thinking her aunts hate each other. Why do you think she is fussing? She has already picked up the naughtiness in your voices."

"Ok, Mom," Kitty whispered, her eyes meeting Ginger's. "Truce, Sis?"

Ginger shrugged, "Sure, why not. We can do this right, can't we, Kitty?"

The younger of the two grinned, "For today, anyhow."

Teddy took the fussing baby from his sister's arms. "Come on, little lady. Let's get you out of the battle zone." She responded with a big smile and reached for the buttons on the bib of his overalls.

Kitty opened the jars of food. After the corn was dumped into a pan and set over the hottest part of the cook stove, she pulled dill pickles out of their jar and sliced them into a pretty cut glass bowl. Then she stacked watermelon pickles in another nice "company" bowl. She lingered for a moment before Mom's china cabinet, admiring the cereal bowls and small plates that had been premiums in containers of Mother's Oats oatmeal.

Mom sampled the escalloped potatoes from where they steamed beside the roast in the oven. She blew on the spoonful to cool it enough for tasting. "M-m-m-m, they are good, Kitty girl. And getting right hot, too. We'll be able to eat in a minute. Put on your coat and go call Pop"

The girl met her mother's eyes and mouthed. "Do I have to?" Mom's answer was a simple nod.

"Where is he?" she asked when she came from the girls' bedroom with her coat. She slipped it on, buttoned it and dug her mittens from her pocket, all the while fighting down the sudden quivering in the pit of her stomach.

"In the shop, I'm sure."

Kitty took her time walking across the yard, avoiding mud patches where snowbanks had recently melted. Globs of smoke sneaking from the shop chimney told her Pop tended a roaring fire to chase away the late March chill.

When she opened the door, the blast of sunshine exposed dust particles in its rays. Kitty closed the door and waited for her eyes to adjust to the dimness of the enclosure.

She saw Pop beside his workbench, sorting bolts and searching for nuts of the right size to fit each bolt. "Come home for a decent meal?"

Kitty shrugged. "Can't beat Mom's cooking."

"Sorry you gave up her goodies for your own fried eggs and taters?"

"No."

"You wouldn't tell me if you were starving from your own cooking."

"How do you know?"

"Your stubborn pride. But I wouldn't let you come back to stay if you did want to." He scooped up a handful of bolts and dumped them into a tin coffee can. "Just the same, any old time you want to come home and fill your belly, you're welcome to do so. Even if there comes a time when there's six little Kittys and Brices." With his remark a rare smile wrinkled his face and hurried Kitty's unfailing blush. Her composure collapsed at this glimpse of his sweeter side. She sniffed, and then stepped over to hug him with the first sincere embrace she could remember ever offering him. Her motion actually smacked of liking the man.

"Your man come along?"

"Yes. Twyla and the baby are here, too, with Frank. He and Brice are relaxing in the living room, waiting for you to come eat dinner with us."

Pop shook his head. "Loafing, and on such a beautiful day to get some work done."

"This is Sunday."

"So what? Ain't got over your religion, have you?"

"If you mean I haven't found anything better than Jesus, no, I haven't."

"You come by your beliefs naturally, from your Ma. I guess it's a weakness for both of you."

"If I'm like Mom when life comes to faith, then I'm glad. Her love of God makes her the fine woman she is."

Pop pulled on his gloves and while buttoning his coat, replied, "I guess you're right about her being fine. But suppose you tell me how. How does faith in God cause her to be like she is?"

"I don't know. Maybe it's because His spirit lives inside her."

"Dinner's ready," she said when he did not reply.

He shut the damper on the stove before they stepped out into the brilliant day. Kitty shivered as Pop pulled the door shut behind them.

They did not speak during the walk across the yard, but as Kitty stepped up on the porch an idea pounded her. Breathlessly, she burst out, "I guess I can explain it a little bit better."

Pop hesitated at the door. "Okay. Let's have your sermon."

Kitty flushed and stammered. "Jesus gave two commandments. The first is to love God with all...with everything you can. And the next is to love your neighbor as yourself. I've never seen anyone who followed those rules any better than Mom. Her love of Jesus makes her wonderful. What do you think?"

"I think I'll think about it," Pop grumbled and the two entered the house.

When the repast was finished and the dishes washed, the women talked in soft voices in the kitchen, enjoying the bright afternoon sunshine sparkling through Mom's kitchen windows. Pop was asleep in his easy chair in the living room. Frank nodded in the rocker, the baby asleep on his lap. Grace and Brice were playing checkers and Ginger was showing off her latest embroidery project to the ladies. Kitty's heart beat with a peace she had so often longed for. She stared at Brice until his warm brown eyes met hers and he smiled as if knowing exactly what she was feeling.

Ginger leaned across the table and whispered to Kitty and Twyla. "There's a new dispatch or whatever you call it, of National Guard soldiers moving in south of Pierre out at Farm Island. You watch Grace. She'll be gone before you know it."

"You're blamed right," sharp-eared Grace answered from her checkers position.

Twyla pretended innocence. "What does she hope to do, be a mascot for some general?"

"Anything, if it will get her a man in a uniform."

"Just what I'm going to do, too. You'll see."

"Rob a bank. You will get a man in a uniform, really quick-like."

"Not permanently, though. And the kind of man in uniform you are referring to is not the kind of uniform she wants hanging in her closet."

"I don't want it hanging in my closet. I want it hanging on my man's back."

"It'll be hanging all right, when you get done chasing him. Hanging in shreds."

"And I won't quit chasing him until I capture him."

"My, you sound like a brash young woman," Mom commented.

Then Kitty finished the subject. "But inside she is shaking like a leaf. I know. Been there, done likewise."

♪ ♪ ♪

In the cheery warmth of their own living room late in the evening, Brice drew Kitty into his arms. "Well, did you have a nice visit?"

"Lovely." Kitty murmured, but sure is nice to be back home."

"This is home now, then?"

"Wherever you are is home for me, Brice. Whether we live in a mansion or a chicken coop, we can make a home, don't you think?"

"Guess so," he whispered against her face, his hands playing absently in her curly brown hair. "I'd rather not have to sleep with those fancy new chickens you brought home today, but maybe someday we'll own a mansion and a chicken coop both."

She giggled, "Do people who live in mansions have chicken coops?"

"How would I know?" He set her lightly on her feet. "Bring me my guitar and we'll sing about our little green valley. We may never put a mansion there, but I think we'll at least get the valley some day, and the chicken coop."

"If God wants us to have those."

"True. And I've an idea when the time is right, He will make them available."

Kitty nodded. Her heart sang with the guitar.

"I hear a Mockingbird, down in the little green valley
He's singing out his heart to welcome me.
There she waits by the garden gate, down in the little green valley.
When I get home again how happy she will be."

THE BEGINNING

Epilogue

It would be ten years before Brice and Kitty moved to their little green valley. They saved and scrimped and did without, then one day he heard the dream ranch near Bad River in Stanley County was for sale.

In the dead of winter he drove north of Murdo to Bad River, crossed it on the Van Metre bridge, drove through Van Metre and crossed the Bad River twice more at the fords, which were frozen over.

He went back to Kitty after his visit, disheartened, and told her there was no way they could possibly buy the ranch.

She refused to give up. She stayed awake for hours, praying and penciling all the details and numbers she could think of. Finally she went to the bedroom, woke up Brice and told him what she had decided.

"If you go back to Mrs. Mathews, offer her the down payment we have saved in the bank and ask if she would take small payments over the years ahead and leave her cattle on the ranch for us to run on shares, the land can one day be ours."

He went back to Bad River with Kitty's offer. Mrs. Mathews agreed, the proper papers were signed and she moved to Denver.

In early March, Brice and Kitty and their three children moved. Bad River was swollen with spring runoff, making the fords impossible to cross, so the caravan had to take the long way around. As they approached the valley, the bare winter hills were the first sight Kitty had of the ranch. She exclaimed, "Oh, hon, what have we done?"

It is said, "If you will stick to the South Dakota gumbo when it's dry, it will stick to you when it's wet."

They stuck. They made it. They thrived.

I was their daughter. But because this is mainly a work of fiction I changed my parents' names and those of their siblings. I only wish had written it while they were still alive. They would have enjoyed my ramblings.

Someday, I may tell you the story of my growing-up years in the Little Green Valley.

THE AUTHOR

Dee LeRoye, also known as Clarice Caldwell Roghair, lives on a ranch on the South Dakota prairie with her husband, Mel.

The couple raised five cowboys and two cowgirls, one of which was adopted. At last count, they have 29 grandchildren and "one in the hopper." Seven great-grandchildren round out the big tables at family gatherings, plus there is another expected this fall. And don't forget two granddaughters-in-love and one grandson-in-love.

Other Christian romance titles available are "The Bronze Cowboy" and "Crossfire" as well as a family history called "Dakota Roghairs." Out of print titles, which could be brought back on demand include "Tame the Flame" and "Meadow Medley."

There is no website at this time, but Dee LeRoye can be found on Facebook. Other contact information is located on page one.